BOOKS BY ROBERT NEWMAN

The Boy Who Could Fly
The Japanese
Merlin's Mistake
The Testing of Tertius
The Shattered Stone
Night Spell
The Case of the Baker Street Irregular
The Case of the Vanishing Corpse
The Case of the Somerville Secret
The Case of the Threatened King

The Case of
the Threatened
King

The Case of
the Threatened
King

by Robert Newman

Atheneum   1982   New York

NewMAN

LIBRARY OF CONGRESS CATALOGING IN PUBLICATION DATA

Newman, Robert.
The case of the threatened king.

SUMMARY: When Sara Wiggins and a friend disappear,
Andrew and Inspector Wyatt's investigation leads to discovery
of a plot against a visiting king.
[1. Mystery and detective stories. 2. Kidnapping—
Fiction. 3. London (England)—Fiction] I. Title.
PZ7.N4857Casg   [Fic]   81-10802
ISBN 0-689-30887-6   AACR2

Published simultaneously in Canada by
McClelland & Stewart, Ltd.
Composition by
American–Stratford Graphic Services, Inc.,
Brattleboro, Vermont
Printed and bound by
Fairfield Graphics, Fairfield, Pennsylvania
Designed by M. M. Ahern
First Edition

For
Jane & Peter Lyon
with
love & thanks

Contents

The Case of the Threatened King

1

The Meetings at Lord's

It was, admittedly, a strange sight. Instead of the white-flanneled figures one usually saw poised on the smooth turf of Lord's, home of the Marylebone Cricket club, there were nine men in the knickerbockers shirts with the team name on the front and colored stockings that Wyatt assured them was the accepted uniform of American baseball players.

Leaning forward with his eyes on the wicket keeper, the Chicago bowler shook his head. After nine innings Andrew knew that he was called the pitcher, not the bowler, and that the player who crouched behind the batsman was called the catcher, not the wicket keeper, but he found it easier to follow and appreciate the game if he used cricket terminology.

And, of course, he was not alone in this. There were probably not more than a dozen spectators in the large crowd who had ever seen a baseball game before, which was why—in spite of the description printed in the program—he heard people all around him speaking of the mid-on, rather than the shortstop, and of a point rather than a fielder. It was also why, when Wyatt—who had been to America and did understand the game—explained one of the plays, everyone within earshot listened.

Now the pitcher nodded, raised his arms in the complicated maneuver that Wyatt had called his windup, and threw the ball. It came at the All-American batter with tremendous speed. The batter swung, there was a loud crack as he lined the ball in a long, hard drive well over the pitcher's head. Almost as if he had expected it, the left fielder turned and raced for the boundary.

It's a good try, thought Andrew, who had always accounted himself a fairly good fielder, but he'll never make it. He can't possibly make it.

But at the last moment, still at a dead run, the Chicago left fielder glanced over his shoulder, threw up his gloved hand and made the catch.

There was a roar from the crowd, and a thunder of applause.

"Oh, well played, sir! Well played indeed!" shouted someone behind Andrew. He turned to smile at the man, who looked like a retired stockbroker, then exchanged delighted glances with Wyatt and with Sara, who sat on the other side of Wyatt.

"And that," said Wyatt, rising, "as our American friends themselves say, is the ball game."

"Is it over?" asked Sara.

Wyatt nodded. "That was the third out in the last half of the ninth inning. Chicago wins four to three. Did you enjoy it?"

"Oh, yes!"

"Andrew?"

"Of course. They really are as keen as mustard, aren't they? I've never seen such running, such smart throws or such brilliant catching."

"They are good; probably the two best teams in America," said Wyatt. "I must say I was a little surprised at the size of the crowd here, but I suspect what the papers had to say about them when they played at the Kennington Oval had something to do with it."

"Tillett! Is that you, Tillett?"

Andrew turned. A boy on the far side of the clubhouse terrace was looking at him.

"Oh, hello, Chadwick," he said.

"I wasn't sure it was you," said Chadwick, threading his way toward him. "If it had been any pair of elevens in the empire, yes. But to come here to see two American baseball teams . . ."

"I know. But you've got to admit that they were something to see."

"Oh, I do. The game's nothing like cricket, but I must say they played jolly well."

"Yes, they did." Sara and Wyatt had paused and were waiting for him. "This is Chadwick," said Andrew. "He's at school with me. Miss Sara Wiggins and Inspector Wyatt."

"How d'ya do?" said Chadwick, bowing to Sara. But his bow was as perfunctory as his glance, for his eyes had gone almost immediately to Wyatt. "Inspector Wyatt of the *Yard?*" he asked, his voice rising slightly.

"I don't know that it warrants the reading you've given it," said Wyatt pleasantly, "but I am at Scotland Yard."

"Oh, I say! I know all about you. I mean . . . Well, it's not as if Tillett talks about you—he won't, even though several of us have asked him, but . . . Just a second. Father!" he called. "Would you come here a moment?"

An almost too-elegantly dressed man, who had been sauntering toward the clubhouse with an older man, hesitated, excused himself, and then came toward them as young Chadwick had done.

"This is Andrew Tillet," said Chadwick. "The chap at school I told you about. This is Miss Wiggins, and this is Inspector Wyatt of Scotland Yard."

Chadwick senior nodded politely to each of them. But when he came to Wyatt, his expression changed somewhat.

"Wyatt," he said. "Didn't you play for Trinity some years ago?"

"Well, yes."

"It was a bit after my time," said Chadwick, "but a cousin of mine was on the eleven with you. Geoffrey Lovell."

"Yes, of course. A very aggressive batsman."

"Yes, he was. Hit a very long ball when he was in form. Trouble was, he wasn't in form very often." Then as Wyatt smiled, "You're at the Yard?"

"Yes."

"I didn't know there were any university men in the Metropolitan Police."

"I don't think there are any others at the moment, but I'm sure there will be in the future."

"I hope so. It would be a very good thing." He looked thoughtfully at Wyatt. "I know that London is your chief bailiwick, but do you ever go outside it? To France, say?"

"A C.I.D. man might go there to pick up a prisoner who was being extradited, but he couldn't do anything else, become involved in a case, for instance. Why do you ask?"

"I'm attached to the embassy in Paris, was called back here for consultation with Sir Roger. But we just got word of something very disturbing that happened there. A shooting."

"At the embassy?"

"Yes."

"One of our people?"

7

"No."

"Well, the French Sûreté is very good. I'm sure they can handle it."

"Probably. But it's not the same thing as working with someone who speaks your language."

"I take it you don't mean that literally."

"No. The fact is that there's a good deal involved. Politically, I mean. And while the French are on our side in it . . ."

"I understand."

"Well, we'd better run along. Nice to meet you, Wyatt. You too, Tillett. And of course you most of all, Miss Wiggins."

"Yes, indeed," said young Chadwick. "Goodbye, sir . . . Miss Wiggins. See you in a few weeks, back at school," he said to Andrew.

"So that's Chadwick," said Sara as he and his father went off.

"Yes," said Andrew. "What did you think of him?"

"He's very nice-looking and has lovely manners, just like his father, but . . ."

"But what?"

"I wonder who was shot?" she said.

"I imagine we'll read about it in the papers tomorrow," said Andrew.

Sara nodded thoughtfully.

Though they had spent some time talking to the Chadwicks, when they left the pavilion they found that there was still a fairly large crowd waiting for their carriages or for hansoms.

"If you don't mind the walk," said Wyatt, "I think we'd have a better chance of picking up a cab on the Wellington Road."

"Of course we don't mind," said Sara. "In fact, I don't know why we need a cab. We can walk home in about fifteen minutes."

"Well," began Wyatt.

"Peter!" said a warm and pleasant voice behind them.

Wyatt turned to face an attractive young woman in a large straw hat who was advancing through the crowd toward them.

"Oh, Harriet. Hello."

"I thought it was you," she said, holding out her hands to him, "but I couldn't be sure until . . . Is that all the greeting I get?" she asked as he took her hands.

"No, of course not," he said, kissing her on both cheeks.

"That's better." She glanced at Sara and Andrew. "Do I know your young friends?"

"I'm not sure. Sara Wiggins and Andrew Tillett. My sister-in-law, Mrs. Francis Wyatt."

"How do you do, ma'am?" said Andrew, as Sara dipped in a curtsey.

"How do you do?" Then, frowning, "Tillett. Aren't you Verna Tillett's son?"

"Yes, ma'am."

"Then we did meet about a year ago at that charity thing of the Marchioness of Medford's. I remember your mother. And I remember Miss Wiggins looking as if she'd stepped out of a Gainsborough."

"And I remember you," said Sara. "You were wearing a fuchsia dress and one of the most beautiful hats I've ever seen."

"Why, thank you, my dear. You're quite right. I still have the dress and hat—they're among my favorites." She turned to Wyatt. "How are you, Peter?"

"Quite well."

"You look well. I heard you'd come up in the world. Or at least in the police hierarchy. Is it true that you're now an inspector at Scotland Yard?"

"Quite true."

"I'm glad. And I must say I like you better in mufti than I did in uniform."

"But not as much as you might in another kind of uniform."

"Now, now! Don't confuse me with certain people who shall be nameless!"

"All right," he said, smiling. "How is Francis?"

"Fine. At least, he says he is. You know he's in India?"

"Yes. I saw it in the *Gazette*. He was posted to the Twelfth Lancers, wasn't he?"

"Yes."

"When will you be joining him?"

"In about three weeks. I have some things to take care of here."

"I'm sure you have." He hesitated. "And father, how's he?"

"Fair."

"Only fair? Is he ill?"

"No, no. He's fine physically. It's just . . . Well, I've been staying with him till I leave. And while he's very pleased about Francis. And about Hal too—he's in Belfast with the Fusiliers, you know—I think he realizes he's going to be quite lonesome after I go."

"I see." He smiled wryly. "Well, *c'est la vie* or *la guerre* or some similar phrase that doesn't sound quite as trite in French as it does in English."

"I know." She sighed. "I wish . . ."

"Don't. Nothing can be done about it."

"I'm not absolutely certain about that. In fact . . ."

She broke off as a shiny black double victoria drew up next to them. The door opened, and a square-shouldered, elderly man with a close-cropped mustache got out.

"All right, my dear," he said to Harriet. "Come along." Then, seeing Wyatt, "You!"

"Hello, father."

"Don't you dare call me that!"

"I'm afraid we're dealing with a biological fact that even an order from you won't change."

"It's a fact I refuse to recognize!"

"Father, this is ridiculous!" said Harriet. "As I tried to point out the other day . . ."

"I told you that it had nothing to do with you. That it was a family affair!"

"Are you saying that though I'm married to your son, your family is not mine?" she asked quietly but firmly.

"I'm saying that I don't want you to interfere in this particular matter." Then, opening the carriage door, "Now are you coming?"

"Go ahead, Harriet," said Wyatt.

"Very well." She kissed him deliberately on the cheek. "It was wonderful to see you again, Peter. I was delighted to hear about your promotion, and now to find you looking so well. Perhaps I'll see you again before I leave for India."

"A nice thought. But under the circumstances . . ."

"Circumstances change." She looked at him levelly and intently for a moment, then smiled. "Goodbye."

"Goodbye, Harriet."

She got into the carriage. The white-mustached gentleman got in after her, slammed the door, and the carriage moved off. Wyatt watched it go, a strange expression on his face. Then he looked down at Sara and Andrew.

"All right, youngsters," he said quietly. "Let's go."

2

The First Disappearance

That Sunday, Wyatt came to the house on Rysdale Road for tea at the express invitation of Andrew's mother. It was not, Verna explained in her note, a quid pro quo—how could you compare even the highest of high teas to an afternoon at Lord's? But she didn't see why she should be denied the pleasure of his company merely because she had been busy when he had extended his invitation to Sara and Andrew.

Wyatt had accepted immediately. "I accept with Alacrity," he wrote, " which happens to be my cousin's name. However he has a bad cold, and I am not sure he can come." And Andrew knew the reason Verna had invited him—and the reason Wyatt had accepted so quickly—was that Sunday was the day when he felt most cut-off from his family and friends and therefore most lonesome.

His reception at the house could not have been warmer, for Andrew's mother was almost as fond of him as the two young people, but in addition he was greatly admired by everyone else there: Sara's mother, Fred the coachman, and even that pillar of propriety, Matson, the butler.

It was Matson who sounded the afternoon's first discordant note. Since it was a warm, sunny day, they were having tea in the garden. The talk had come round to the baseball game they had seen several days before and, leaving the table briefly, Wyatt was demonstrating the complicated contortions of the Chicago pitcher during his windup, when Matson came out of the house.

"I beg your pardon, madam," he said. "General Wyatt is here."

Frowning, Verna looked from him to Wyatt, who had become very still, then back to Matson again.

"General Wyatt?"

"Yes, madam."

"Does he want me or Inspector Wyatt?"

"I believe he'd like to speak to the inspector. The first thing he asked me was whether he was here."

"Ask him to come out here."

Bowing, Matson went back into the house. Again Verna glanced at Wyatt, who had dropped the croquet ball he was holding. Though his face was expressionless, it was clear that he was surprised—which was no surprise to Sara and Andrew, for they had long been aware of the strained relations between him and his father. As a matter of fact, they had been present at another encounter between the two some time before when Wyatt was still a constable. He had, at that time, explained the reasons for his father's attitude; the general was outraged because Wyatt had become an ordinary policeman instead of going into the army as his two older brothers had done. And apparently the fact that he was no longer a constable but an inspector in the C.I.D. made no difference to the general.

When Matson returned, it was clear that the general was under considerable strain. Though as carefully dressed as he had been at Lord's, his face had lost a good deal of its color and his eyes much of their challenge.

"I apologize for this intrusion, Miss Tillett," he said, bowing to Verna. "I'm not sure if you remember me . . ."

"Of course I do," said Verna. "We met at the Marchioness of Medford's about a year ago. Miss Wiggins here and my son Andrew were with me at the time."

"I remember them," said the general. "And I believe I saw them again the other day with my son Peter at Lord's."

"You did. Can I offer you some tea?"

"You're very kind, but no thank you. The fact is that I would like to talk to Peter about a matter of some urgency."

"By all means," said Verna. "Inspector, why don't

you take the general to the sitting room? Matson will see that you're not disturbed."

"Thank you," said Wyatt. "This way, sir."

He led the general into the house, held the door of the sitting room open for him, followed him in and shut the door after them.

"First of all, how did you know where I was?" he asked.

"I stopped by at your rooms. Your landlady told me you were here."

Wyatt nodded. "I always leave word where I can be reached in case the Yard wants me. You said you wanted to see me about something urgent?"

"If it weren't urgent, you know very well I wouldn't have approached you—especially on a Sunday. It's your sister-in-law, Harriet. She's disappeared."

"Disappeared?"

"Yes."

"When was this?"

"I'm not sure whether she left late last night or early this morning. She's been staying with me since Francis went to India. She went to the opera last night with a friend, said good night to me when she got home and went into her room. When she didn't appear at breakfast this morning, I thought she must be tired or not feeling well. By noon I became a little concerned, knocked at her door. When there was no answer, I went in and found this."

He gave Wyatt an envelope. Wyatt opened it, took out the note inside and read it.

Dear General, (it said)
   The fact that I call you that and not Father should tell you something about the way I feel. If it does not, perhaps the fact that I am going away will. Don't try to find me, for you won't be able to; I doubt if all of Scotland Yard could. As to what you should tell Francis or anyone else who might be interested, say merely that I became tired of sitting like Patience on a monument, smiling at grief.
                                                                      Harriet

Wyatt read it through a second time, then asked, "What did she mean about the way she felt? How did she feel?"

"I've no idea."

"She never discussed it with you, told you that she was unhappy and why?"

"No."

"How did she feel about going to India?"

The general's face became even more bleak. "I don't know. I always believed that she loved Francis, that they had a good marriage and that she was anxious to go out and join him, but . . . You think that's why she disappeared, because she didn't want to go?"

"I'm not sure. I'd like to see her room, see if there's anything there that tells me anything."

"My carriage is outside."

Matson opened the front door for them. Wyatt asked him to tell Miss Tillett that he was leaving and convey his regrets to her, then he joined the general in the double victoria. They sat there, side by side, in silence as the carriage went down the driveway and over toward Regent's Park. But though they said nothing, Wyatt thought about many things, most of them dealing with the past rather than the present; of the times when his father had seemed like the most wonderful man in the world to him and the times when he had seemed like a stubborn, bigoted monster. And from the expression on the general's face, it's probable that his thoughts paralleled those of his son.

Wyatt knew that the general had rented two floors of a small house near Robert Street on the east side of Regent's Park, but he had done so after their breach, and Wyatt had never been there. He looked at the house with some interest now as they drew up in front of it. The steps that led up to the door were scrubbed and the brass bellpull gleamed like a sergeant-major's buttons. The general opened the door with a latch key, led the way down a hall past a sitting room and opened another door.

"This is her room," he said.

Wyatt went in and looked around. The room, large

and high-ceilinged, overlooked a small garden and was light and pleasant. There was a bed and chest of drawers against one wall. Facing it was a fireplace with an ornate marble mantel. There was a desk between the two windows that looked out onto the garden, and nearby was a large, open steamer trunk.

"Where did you find the note?" asked Wyatt.

"Here," said the general, indicating the mantel. "It was leaning against the clock."

Wyatt nodded, walked over to the desk. Besides a pen, ink and several sheets of the same paper on which the note had been written, there was a book with a bookmark in it. He picked it up. It was a well-worn copy of William Blake's poems and the bookmark was inserted between two pages in the *Songs of Innocence.*

"Did she like Blake?" he asked.

"You mean the poet? I've no idea. I know she read a good deal, but I don't know what."

Wyatt now went over to the trunk. "Do you know what clothes she took with her."

"No. I believe she took only one bag with her, a not very large portmanteau."

"She probably took that because she could carry it herself." He was still studying the trunk. "She seems to have left all her tropical, Indian things here."

"What does that mean?"

"I'm not sure yet." He turned to face the general. "How long have she and Francis been married?"

"A little over three years."

"As I recall, they met at a house party in Gloucestershire."

"Yes."

"What was her maiden name?"

"Darrell. Harriet Darrell."

"What family does she have?"

"None anymore. When she met Francis, she was an orphan, living with an aunt in Bath. The aunt died about a year ago."

"She and Francis were married here in London, weren't they?"

"Yes. At St. George's."

"Where did she stay before the wedding? At a hotel?"

"No. I believe she stayed at some club or other." The general had been exhibiting more and more impatience with Wyatt's questions. "Does any of this have anything to do with her disappearance?"

"I'm not sure. The fact is, sir, that we're faced with a bit of a problem here."

"What sort of problem?"

"Well, from the note she left and the look of the room, it's clear that she's gone away of her own accord. That means there's no legal reason for the police to come in on the case. After all, one should be able to go where one wants."

"Even though it means the end of a marriage and perhaps the end of a career? Because you know what it will do to Francis if she's not on that boat when it arrives in India, don't you?

"I think so."

"And you still say you're not going to do anything about it?"

Wyatt looked at him thoughtfully, at the new signs of age that had appeared on the general's face, and knew what it had cost the man to come to him of all people for help.

"I never said I wasn't going to do anything about it, Father. I was merely explaining the official, police position to you. Let me look into it, and I'll get in touch with you as soon as I've something to tell you."

3

The Second Disappearance

When Matson came back and told them that Wyatt had left with the general, it was the direct and natural Sara who put what they were all thinking into words.

"None of our beeswax of course, but I wonder what that was all about."

"It must have been something pretty important," said Andrew.

"Important? I wouldn't have thought there was anything in the world that would have made him come here looking for Wyatt after the way he acted at Lord's!"

"What happened at Lord's?" asked Verna.

Sara and Andrew exchanged glances and then told her.

"I see," said Verna. "Of course I knew that there were problems there and why."

"Do you think Wyatt will tell us what it was about?" asked Sara.

"I doubt it," said Verna. "And, I don't think I'd ask him. It's probably a family or a personal matter."

Sara sighed. "All right. I won't ask."

It was two days before any of them saw Wyatt again, and when they did, they then had something much more important on their minds than the general's unexpected visit. These were the circumstances:

It was late afternoon, and Verna and Andrew were in the sitting room, reading. Verna, reading a play script that had been sent her, finished it and dropped it on the table next to her.

"No good?" asked Andrew.

"Oh, it's a perfectly good play—well-written and well put together—but the part they want me to play is exactly like Rowena in *The Squire's Daughter*."

"That's probably why Harrison sent it to you."

"It is. But I've told him a dozen times I won't play an ingenue again. I'm not only too old for it, the idea of doing the same thing again makes me ill."

"I can understand that, but I don't think you're too old to play ingenues—not at all."

"You're as bad as Harrison. What are you reading?"

"One of Layard's books."

"Layard?"

"Austin Henry Layard, the antiquarian. Or archeologist as they're starting to call them."

"Weren't you reading one of his books the last time you were down?"

"Yes. That was rather general. This is about his discoveries in the ruins of Nineveh and Babylon."

"Sounds interesting. And also like something your friend Lord Somerville might be involved in. Didn't he have a dig somewhere near there?"

"Yes. It was he who suggested that I read Layard. He said he was not just one of the first, he was one of the best Assyriologists. But . . ."

There was a light tap on the door, and Annie, the parlormaid, came in, trim in her white cap and apron, wanting to know if they would like their tea now. Verna, who hadn't realized it was five o'clock, asked if Sara was home from dancing school yet and, learning she wasn't, said they'd wait until she did get home—which should be soon since she was a bit late already.

As Annie left, Andrew stood up and stretched.

"I've been indoors most of the afternoon. I think I'll walk over there."

"To the school?"

"Yes. Though I'm sure I'll run into Sara long before I get there."

"Right, darling. Go ahead. I want to write Harrison a note about the play."

Fred, the coachman, was in the stable yard polishing the side lights of the landau when Andrew came out of the house. He whistled shrilly, jerking his head at the carriage, which was his way of asking if he was wanted.

Andrew shook his head, walked down the driveway and right on Rysdale Road toward Wellington Road.

London is, of course, many small villages that have grown together but have still managed, in most cases, to preserve their own identity. And at this particular hour St. John's Wood was most like itself: quiet, respectable and suburban. Since it was late in the day, the sun cast long shadows, gilding the spire of the Church of St. John and the roof of the Hospital of St. John and St. Elizabeth. Two cabbies sat on a bench in front of The Red Dragon, pints in their hands, while their horses munched their evening oats. A dark green City Atlas bus rattled by down Wellington Road on its way to London Bridge, and as Andrew crossed the street behind it, the Marchioness of Medford's carriage turned into Rysdale Road and the coachman, a friend of Fred's, touched his cockaded hat with his whip in greeting.

Entering the narrower, shaded streets west of Wellington Road, Andrew found himself thinking about the conversation he had just had with his mother. What he had not told her was what Wyatt had said about his new interest in archeology. He had smiled when he had first heard about it and, when pressed, he asked Andrew if it had not occurred to him that it was another form of detective work.

"They hunt for potsherds and artifacts," he said, "and use their intelligence, their reasoning powers, to make sense out of them, understand a civilization, just as a detective puts clues and evidence together to understand a crime."

When Andrew had looked a little startled, Wyatt had laughed and said he was joking. And, while he may have been, Andrew had realized that there was a good deal of truth in what he said. That one of the reasons he had been so attracted to archeology was that it did bear such a resemblance to the work the man he liked and admired so much was doing.

He was still musing about careers, wondering whether he'd rather be a famous archeologist or a famous detective when he reached the dancing school, which was in a stucco villa set back behind a somewhat neglected garden.

It had taken him a little over ten minutes to walk to the school, and he was a little surprised that he had not run into Sara on the way for, though he knew she occasionally stayed there until four-thirty, he did not recall her ever having been this late before.

He tugged at the bellpull, heard it jangle inside, and a few moments later the door was opened by a maid whose cap was not quite straight and who didn't seem to be much older than he was.

"Yes, sir?" she said. It was fairly obvious from the smear of jam at the corner of her mouth that he had taken her away from her tea. She seemed surprised when he asked for Sara.

"Why, she's not here, sir."

"She's not?"

"Who is it, Katie?" called a voice from somewhere inside the cavernous reaches of the house.

"A young gentleman asking for Miss Sara Wiggins."

Footsteps approached, the door opened wider, and Miss Fizdale, a thin woman in her late forties, appeared behind the maid.

"You're Andrew Tillett, are you not?"

"Yes, Miss Fizdale."

"I remember you from the spring dance recital. That must have been the last time you were home on holiday." Then, as he nodded, "But Sara's not here. She left some time ago."

"Oh. Well, I must have missed her walking over here."

"Yes, you must have. But even then . . ." She turned. "Do you know what time Sara left, Miss Caroline?"

Miss Caroline, shorter and plumper than Miss Fizdale, appeared beside her. Andrew didn't know her last name. All he knew about her was that she wore pince-nez and a high-necked dark dress like Miss Fizdale and that she played the piano for the school. She was clutching a napkin, so apparently the two ladies had been at tea also.

"She left at the usual time—four o'clock. You mean she's not home yet?"

"She wasn't when I left. She probably went somewhere with one of the other girls."

27

"Probably," said Miss Fizdale. "Though I must say I don't approve of that—going off without letting anyone at home know. Tell her mother—or yours—to speak very severely to her about it!"

"Yes, Miss Fizdale. I will."

He left. It was interesting that Miss Fizdale had mentioned his mother as well as Sara's; interesting but not surprising. Because it was Verna who had made the arrangements for Sara to attend the dancing school, and of course it was she who was paying for it. But where was Sara? *Had* she gone off with one of the other girls? Or had she gone home by a different route from the one she usually took, so that he had missed her? In any case, she'd undoubtedly be home by the time he got there.

But she wasn't. Verna looked up from the note she was writing when he came in.

"Well, that was quick," she said.

"I hurried a bit. Is Sara here?"

"Why, no. Wasn't she at the school?"

"No. Miss Fizdale said she left at the usual time, about four o'clock. Perhaps she went off with another girl, one of her friends."

"She wouldn't have done that without letting her mother know."

"Maybe she did."

Verna shook her head. "If she had, Mrs. Wiggins would have said something about it when we told Annie we were going to wait for our tea." She looked thoughtfully at Andrew and stood up. "I'll ask her to make sure but, in the meantime, call Fred. I'll go over to the school with you."

He nodded, went out and had Fred bring the carriage around. They both looked at Verna when she came out of the house, wearing a hat and pulling on her gloves.

"She didn't say anything to her mother. Take us to Miss Fizdale's, Fred."

"Yes, ma'am." He shook the reins, started the horses down the driveway.

"Is she worried?" asked Andrew. "Mrs. Wiggins, I mean?"

"Not really. I told her not to be."

"But you are."

"A little. This isn't like Sara."

"No, it's not."

They didn't tell Fred to hurry, but they didn't have to. He put the horses into a fast trot, and a few minutes later Andrew was tugging at the bellpull for the second time. Miss Fizdale must have looked out the window when she heard the carriage stop for when the little maid opened the door again her mistress was with her.

"Good afternoon, Miss Tillett," she said. "Are you here about Sara too?"

"Yes. She's still not home and she didn't say anything to her mother about going anywhere. Are you sure she left at the time she usually does?"

"Well, I didn't actually see her leave myself . . ."

"I did," said Miss Caroline who had joined Miss Fizdale again. "And she left when all the other pupils did, just a few minutes after four."

"Alone?"

"Yes. I came out to get one of the girls who was staying on for some special work with Miss Fizdale—Maria Milanovitch—and Sara was talking to her. When I said Miss Fizdale was waiting for her—Miss Maria, I mean— Sara left." She was crumpling a handkerchief, dabbing at her mouth with it. "You don't think anything's happened to her, do you?"

"Well, we are a little concerned."

"I'm sure there's no reason to be," said Miss Fizdale without much conviction. "I'm sure she'll turn up very soon."

"I'm not as sure of that as you are," said Verna. "But thank you."

She and Andrew went back down the steps.

"I don't like this," said Andrew.

"I don't either. If I were a proper citizen of our time, believing that this is the best of all possible worlds, I'd say, 'This is London, center of the empire and a place of law and order. I'm sure nothing has happened to her and I'm not even going to think about it, much less worry about it until . . . let's say dinnertime.' But, as you know, I'm not a proper, average citizen, and I don't mind creating a disturbance when I think there's a good reason for it. So—" She stepped into the landau. "Fred, take us to Scotland Yard."

"Yes, ma'am," said Fred, and closing the door, he got back into the box, shook the reins and started the horses south toward the Yard.

"Are we going to talk to Inspector Wyatt?"

"Yes. I suppose we could go to the local police, but I believe in going to the top if I can. And besides, he knows Sara."

"Yes. But it's getting late. He may not be at the Yard."

"If he's not, I'm sure they'll know where to reach him."

But apparently Wyatt had not left yet. The desk sergeant wrote Verna's name on a slip of paper, gave it to a constable and suggested that she and Andrew sit down on the benches on the far side of the reception room. A few moments later Wyatt came down, followed by Sergeant Tucker.

"Hello," he said. Then after a quick glance at her face, "I gather this isn't a social call."

"No. We're worried about Sara."

"Oh? What happened?"

Verna told him, and Wyatt listened intently.

"What's the name of the woman who runs the dancing school?"

"Miss Fizdale."

"Address?"

She told him, and Sergent Tucker wrote it down in his omnipresent notebook.

"All right. Go home and tell Mrs. Wiggins there's no reason to be concerned—at least, not yet. The sergeant or I will stop by sometime this evening and let you know if we've anything to report."

"Thank you."

Mrs. Wiggins was in the sitting room with Verna and Andrew at about ten o'clock that night when Matson opened the door and announced Wyatt. The inspector studied their faces, they studied his, and all of them knew the answer at once. Nevertheless, the questions were asked.

"I gather there's been no word from her," said Wyatt.

"No," said Verna. "Have you found out anything?"

"No. Sergeant Tucker stopped by at the Wellington Road police station, and between us we made enquiries at the local hospitals. She's not at any of them, and the local police don't know anything." Then, as Mrs. Wiggins covered her face and Verna put her arms around her, "I'm not going to say you mustn't worry, Mrs. Wiggins. I don't know how you can help it. But I'm sure I don't have to tell you how I feel about Sara. If it's humanly possible to find her, get her back safely, we'll do it."

4

Sara Alone

Some time before that, at about six o'clock, Sara regained consciousness; not all at once, but slowly and painfully. Her head ached, her mouth was dry, and when she opened her eyes, everything was blurry. She blinked and gradually her vision cleared. She was in a strange room, one she had never seen before; and when she tried to sit up and study it, a wave of nausea came over her and she slumped back and closed her eyes again to keep from throwing up. The nausea passed, and opening her eyes, she sat up very slowly and carefully.

The room she was in was small and bare. It was probably an attic room, for the ceiling pitched down sharply to two dormer windows. There were two iron cots in the room. She was lying on one of them. The other had an old mattress on it but no sheets or blanket. There was a door to her left. To her right was a window that looked out over some roofs. There was a chest of drawers next to the window with a looking glass on it and, in the corner of the room, a wash stand with a pitcher and basin. The only other piece of furniture in the room was a rickety wooden chair.

From the looks of the furniture, all of which was old and decrepit, and from the fact that the room was in the attic, it was clear that it had once been a servant's room. As to where it was and how she had gotten there, Sara had no idea. Sitting up a little straighter and covering her eyes with her hand, she tried to concentrate and see what she could remember.

Dancing school—she could remember that, who had been there and what they had been doing, even the fact that Miss Caroline had had a coughing fit in the middle of the schottische. When she had left, she had started to walk back to Rysdale Road, following the same route she always did. As she went around the corner, a four-wheeler drew up, the driver knotted the reins around the whipsocket, got down from the box and came toward her. He was a big man, almost as big as Sergeant Tucker, and he was heavily bearded. He wore a coachman's coat and top hat, but his boots and breeches looked military. Sara had a feeling that he was a foreigner before he said anything to her, and once he did, there was no question about it.

"Excuse please, missy," he said with a guttural voice and with a decided accent. "Where I find . . ." Whatever it was he wanted to find sounded like *hobagob*.

"I beg your pardon?"

The big man looked at her unhappily.

"If you come here," he said, nodding toward the four-wheeler," *he* tell you."

Evidently whoever was in the four-wheeler spoke better English than he did.

She walked over to it, the coachman opened the door, and as she leaned forward to talk to whoever was inside, a strong hand clutched her by the back of the neck and another clapped a damp cloth over her mouth and nose. As she drew in her breath to scream, she smelled something sweetish. The damp cloth muffled her scream, and at the same time, she realized that she shouldn't breathe in whatever it was that saturated the cloth. But by then it was too late; her senses were starting to slip away.

"No," she remembered thinking, "this can't be happening. It can't."

But of course it had happened. She dropped the hand that had been covering her eyes. Her mouth was dry and had a vile taste in it. She wondered if there was any water in the pitcher on the washstand. As she started to get up and see, she heard footsteps coming up the stairs. She immediately closed her eyes and dropped flat again, as if she were still unconscious. The lock clicked, the door opened and closed, and footsteps came into the room.

She opened her eyes cautiously, peered out through

her long lashes. A man stood at the foot of the cot looking down at her, not the coachman, another man.

"You," he said, "wake up!" He spoke much better English than the coachman, but he had a decided accent, too.

Sara did not move. Bending down, he took her by the shoulder and shook her, not roughly but firmly and decisively.

Slowly Sara opened her eyes. Though only of medium height, the man who looked down at her was, in his way, even more striking than the big coachman had been. Broad-shouldered and erect, he was well-dressed, wearing a frock coat and striped trousers. And while the coachman had been heavily bearded, he was not only clean-shaven, but his head was shaved as well, and he was studying Sara through a single eyeglass that was clamped in his left eye.

"How do you feel?" he asked.

Some deep-rooted instinct took over and, without being completely sure why she did it, Sara scrapped all the training Andrew's mother had given her in proper speech and reverted to an earlier style, the speech she had learned and used in Dingell's Court, off Edgeware Road.

"I feels awful!" she said in her broadest Cockney. " 'Oo are you?"

He stiffened. "I'm Colonel Kosta," he said, frowning down at her. "Who are you?"

"I'm Screamer."

"Who?"

"That's what they calls me. Me real name is Sara. Sara Wiggins."

"Wiggins?"

"Yus. Where is this place? Why'd you bring me here? And—"

"Never mind that. Where do you live?"

"Rysdale Road."

"And your name is Wiggins?"

"I told you it was."

He continued to stare down at her, scowling so fiercely that the top edge of his monocle disappeared under his eyebrow. Then, turning abruptly, he strode to the door and pulled it open.

"Zerko!" he called.

There were heavy footsteps on the stairs; the coachman came into the room, drew himself up and saluted the colonel.

Looking at him with cold fury, Kosta jerked his head at Sara and asked him a question in a guttural language that seemed to be mostly consonants. Startled, the coachman looked at Sara, nodded and answered with a single word. Kosta asked him what sounded like another question, and this time the coachman's answer was longer and more involved. Barking out a single phrase, the colonel slapped him across the face. The coachman did not blink or move. Then, when the colonel said something else that seemed to be an order, he saluted again, turned and left the room. His face still flushed and angry, Kosta said, "Why did you say you did not feel well?"

"I feels sick. And me head hurts. And besides, I'm thirsty."

"There's water in the pitcher. Zerko filled it a little while ago, so it's fresh." He walked to the door and opened it. "I'll be back."

He closed and locked the door. Sara waited until she heard his footsteps going down the stairs, then she swung her feet over the side of the bed and stood up. Another wave of nausea came over her and she swayed dizzily, had to close her eyes. She kept them closed for a moment, then when she felt better, she went over to the wash-stand. There was a mug next to the basin. She filled it, drank and splashed some of the water on her face; then she began walking around the room, studying it while she tried to decide where she was and why she had been brought there.

The setting sun was shining in through the window opposite the door. That meant it faced west. Bending down, she looked out the other, smaller dormer windows. Across a narrow alley was the blank brick wall of building that was taller than the one she was in. She looked down. The alley, some four stories below her, was cobbled and there was no sign of movement in it. If the single window to her right faced west, the dormer windows must face south. Over the distant sound of traffic—

horses' hoofs, the clatter of iron-rimmed wheels—she heard the chuffing of a boat engine and a hooting whistle. That and the faintly salty smell blended with the smell of sewage meant that the house was close to the Thames, some distance from St. John's Wood and the part of London she knew best.

She went back to the window that faced west. The roof it overlooked was only a few feet below it, but there were bars on the window so she could not get out that way. Beyond the roof, about twenty feet away, was a fairly wide street. Looking down and at an angle, she could see a good-sized section of it. The houses that lined it seemed neat and fashionable, and so did the man and woman who strolled by on the far side of it. If she screamed, Sara wondered, would they hear her? Probably not. And even if they did, it was not likely that they would be able to locate her, decide where she was, certainly not before Colonel Kosta or Zerko, the coachman, heard her and came back into the room to gag her or silence her more permanently.

She stepped back from the window. The looking glass on the chest of drawers was mounted on a stand with a side pivot and she adjusted it so that she could look at herself. Was it likely that they might silence her permanently, in other words, kill her? She studied herself thoughtfully. She couldn't say, 'No, that's impossible.' That's what she had said when Zerko or someone had clapped the wet pad to her mouth and nose, and look at where she was. What happened would depend on why they had kidnapped her and brought her here, and so far she didn't know why.

She walked back to the cot that had a blanket and pillow on it and stretched out.

Well, I'm in something up to my khyber this time, she thought. Sara alone, in durance vile. She wasn't sure where she'd gotten that phrase or even exactly what it meant (Andrew would know: he knew almost everything), but she was pretty sure it meant that you were a prisoner. And that's what she was, all right. Or was she a captive? What was the difference between a prisoner and a captive?

A much more important question was, why? Why had she been kidnapped and brought here? Was it for money, ransom? She suddenly realized why, without really thinking about it, she had decided to play the role of a not very bright—and certainly not very well-educated—Cockney girl. If she were not very bright, they'd be less likely to watch her carefully, which meant she'd have a better chance of getting help or escaping. And of course, if she were no one special, they couldn't expect anyone to come up with any whacking big ransom to get her back.

This brought up another interesting question—or rather the original and most important one in another form. *Did* they know who she was? From the way Colonel Kosta had reacted—and the way he had questioned Zerko—she had a feeling that perhaps they didn't. She'd have to wait and see. But in the meantime, what she *wasn't* going to do was worry. Because so far the colonel had no idea of how smart she was, and one way or another, she was sure she was going to get out of the predicament she was in.

Lying there on the cot, she must have fallen asleep, for when she heard voices and footsteps on the stairs again, the room was dark. She sat up when the door was unlocked and opened. Zerko came in carrying an oil lamp. He was followed by Colonel Kosta and another man and woman. Kosta remained at the door, but the man and woman advanced to the foot of the cot and looked down at Sara. The woman, in her own way, was just as striking as Zerko or the colonel. It was difficult to tell her age for, though by no means young, her face was so heavily powdered that it looked like a white mask. Her hair, piled high on her head, was bright red and was so elaborately curled that Sara was convinced it was a wig. Her eyes were dark and glittering, she wore a mulberry velvet dress and carried a silver-headed ebony cane.

She jerked her head, and the man, who had been standing a little behind her, took the lamp from Zerko and set it on the table between the two cots. As he did, Sara got her first good look at him. He was shorter and slighter than the woman, wore a nondescript dark suit with a kingsman, a brightly colored scarf, around his neck instead of a collar and tie. There was something rodent-like about him, for his face was narrow and his eyes dark and set close together. Though he seemed to be smiling, his eyes were as cold and hard as jet beads.

"All right, duck," said the woman in a flat, rasping voice. "Who are you?"

"I'm Screamer."

"Screamer?"

"That's what they calls me. Who are you?"

"Never mind who I am or what they calls you. What's your name?"

"Sara. Sara Wiggins."

"And where do you live?"

"Twenty-three Rysdale Road."

"Come off it! What'd a bit of fluff like you be doing living on Rysdale Road?"

"Who's a bit of fluff? I'm a good gel, I am!"

"Are you?"

"Yes, I am!"

"But you know what a bit of fluff is."

"Sure I do. I used to live over at Dingell's Court, off Edgeware Road."

"That's more like it. What are you doing on Rysdale Road?"

"I told you, living there. Me mum's the housekeeper."

"Oh? Is that where you got the duds you're wearing?"

"Yes. They're hand-me-downs the lady we work for gets from her friends."

"So you work there, too?"

"Yes. I'm the tweenie."

"What about this dancing school over near the Wellington Road—Miss Fizdale's?"

"What about it?"

"Do you go there?"

"Sometimes. The missis we work for don't know it, but I wants to learn, not just how to dance, but how to talk and act like a lydy and they teaches you that there. So when we've a bit put by, I goes there."

The woman with the red wig stared at her fixedly for a moment.

"Well, Sam?" she asked finally. The rat-faced man nodded once. "I think so, too. She's what she says she is," she said to the colonel. "You've nabbed the wrong girl."

"You're sure?"

"Sure as water's wet." Then as he swore vehemently in his unknown foreign tongue, "Well, it serves you right. I told you that I wanted to do the whole job, and you thought it was too much, thought you could do it yourself. Well, now that you've mucked this part of it, I want what I said *and* another two hundred quid."

"Two hundred *more?*"

"Yes."

He studied her, frowning, then nodded. "All right."

"Good-oh. Come on, Sam." And she started for the door, limping a little and leaning on her ebony stick.

" 'arf a mo'!" said Sara. "What about me?"

"What about you?"

"What's going to happen to me?"

"Nothing, ducky. We'll have to keep you here for a few days, but you'll be all right."

"Oh, I will, will I? Well, thanks for nothing! In the meantime, don't I even get anything to eat?"

"Of course you do. The sergeant here," she jerked her head at Zerko, "will bring you something."

"Besides being hungry, I'm scared of the dark. How about leaving the lamp?"

"All right, ducky. We'll do that too. Nighty-night and pleasant dreams." And she went out, followed by her companion, Sam, by Zerko and the colonel.

5

The Ransom Note

The church clock began striking the hour, and when it had struck four times, the grandfather clock in the upstairs hall began striking. Andrew, sitting in the front parlor with his mother and Mrs. Wiggins, did not have to count the strokes to know that it was ten o'clock. He had been very much aware of the time after Inspector Wyatt and Sergeant Tucker had left the night before and even more aware of it since he had gotten up that morning.

He glanced at Mrs. Wiggins. Sitting well forward in her chair, she had stiffened when the church clock began striking, listening intently, as she had to every sound that they had heard since Andrew and his mother had come down early that morning. And since her bed had not been slept in, it was very likely that she had been

45

sitting there, reacting to every sound, for most of the night.

Though her face was calm, there were new lines in it, and Andrew had some sense of how she must feel from the way he felt. In the beginning, though it was clear that something was wrong, he had hoped that it was nothing serious; that there would be a knock on the door and Sara would come in with some explanation as to where she had been. When Wyatt and Tucker had told them that she was not at any of the likely hospitals, that hope had disappeared. Something definitely *had* happened to Sara, and it was now a matter of finding out exactly what. (Was it possible that they never *would* find out? That she was just gone, gone forever?)

Andrew got up, went to the window and looked out. No, that wasn't possible! Even though he knew that that sort of thing did happen, it wasn't going to happen to Sara. It couldn't. Too many people cared too much about her.

"How about something to eat now, Mrs. Wiggins?" asked Verna. When they had first come downstairs, she had talked with Matson and determined that Mrs. Wiggins had not had any breakfast.

"Thank you, ma'am, but not right now."

"If you're waiting until we hear something, it may be quite a while, and you've got to keep your strength up as well as your spirits."

"I know that, but I couldn't manage anything just yet."

"All right, Mrs. Wiggins."

Andrew turned and looked at her, exchanged glances with his mother, then looked out of the window again. Though their house was set well back from Rysdale Road, the parlor windows were high enough that Andrew could see over the hedge, see most of the street. No one was walking up or down it, and no carriage, hansom or four-wheeler had gone by for several minutes. The only movement anywhere was by the mason on the scaffolding in front of the Fulton house across the street. He had been there when Andrew had first looked out of the window that morning, standing on the scaffolding with his back to the street and chipping away at the flaking and discolored stucco with a hammer and chisel.

There was the sound of voices from the back of the house, and footsteps came down the hall toward the parlor. Andrew turned, puzzled. They were a man's footsteps, but they weren't Matson's; he walked much more quietly and diffidently. The door opened, and Wyatt came in followed by Sergeant Tucker.

"Good morning," he said. Andrew had a feeling that he had not had much sleep the night before, but he did not look it. He was freshly shaved and his clothes were unwrinkled.

"Good morning," said Verna.

"How did you get in?" asked Andrew.

"Back way," said Tucker. "Through the mews and the stable."

"Why?"

"We didn't want anyone to know we were here," said Wyatt. He looked at Andrew's mother and then at Mrs. Wiggins. "Any word? Anything?"

"No, Inspector," said Mrs. Wiggins. "Nothing."

"Has the morning post been delivered?"

"Yes. There was nothing there."

"Well, that doesn't mean anything. It's still pretty early."

"Have you had breakfast, Inspector?" asked Andrew's mother.

"Yes. The sergeant and I had it together some time ago. I assume you did."

"Andrew and I did, but not Mrs. Wiggins. She says she can't eat anything."

"Oh." Wyatt looked at the housekeeper. "You really should make yourself eat, Mrs. Wiggins," he said gently. "I know what a bad time this is for you, but . . ." He broke off as a bell jangled in the kitchen. "Is that the front door?"

"Yes," said Mrs. Wiggins, her eyes widening.

"Let Matson open the door," said Wyatt to Tucker, who had already started out, "but stand by."

"Yes, Inspector," said Tucker, going out.

They waited, heard the front door open. There was a brief exchange between Matson and someone else, a perfunctory knock on the sitting room door, and Matson came in with an envelope on a silver tray.

"A note for Mrs. Wiggins," he said.

"I'll take it," said Wyatt. He opened the envelope, took out a hair ribbon and a note, read the note and said, "Who brought it, Matson?"

"A boy, sir."

"What kind of boy?"

"A rather dirty one, sir. A street urchin."

"What happened to him?"

"He gave me the note, started to leave. The sergeant let him get almost to the street, then called to him. I think—" The front door closed, and Matson looked out into the hall. "Yes. Here they come."

He stepped aside, and Tucker and a boy came into the room. He was probably about ten years old, though if he was, he was small for his age. His hair, closely cropped, stood up in spikes on top of his head. His boots were cracked and full of holes, and his ragged trousers were held up by a piece of rope. But though his face was far from clean, it was bright and alert.

"Did you deliver this note?" Wyatt asked him, holding it up.

"Yus, guv'ner."

"What's your name?"

"Harry."

"Can you tell me where you got the note, Harry? Who gave it to you?"

"Yes, but it won't do you much good."

"Why not?"

"Are you a busy?"

"Yes. How did you know?"

"You wouldn't be asking me all those questions if you wasn't. Besides, I think *he* is," he said, nodding toward Sergeant Tucker, who was in plain clothes. "He used to be a copper."

"How do you know that?" asked Tucker.

"Because I done your boots a couple of times when you was in uniform."

"Wait a minute. I thought you looked familiar. You used to black boots in front of the Underground station."

"I still do."

"Will you tell us where you got that note, Harry?"

"Sure, guv'ner. It happened a little while ago. A carriage pulls up and the charley-boy inside asks me if I want to make two bob. I says sure and starts to look in, but he says, 'Never mind that. Stay where you are.' And he hands me the envelope and two bob and says, 'Take this to Twenty-three Rysdale Road and no tricks because someone'll be watching you and if you try anything on you'll get your neck broke.' So that's what I done. I brung it here."

"And you never got a look at the man who gave it to you?"

"No. He was sitting back in the corner, and when I sees he don't want me to lamp him, I don't try."

"You said he was in a carriage. Was it a private carriage or a cab?"

"Neither. It wasn't no cab because it didn't have no number on it. And it wasn't smart enough to be private. I think it was a livery carriage."

"What about the coachman? Did you get a look at him?"

"Just from the back. He never turned around. But he was a big boyo."

"Can you tell me anything at all about the man in the carriage? Was he a toff, for instance?"

"Nohow! He talked about like me."

"Well, that's a help. Do you think you'd know the carriage if you saw it again?"

"I might."

"All right. I'm Inspector Wyatt. If you see the carriage again and you can find out anything about it or the man who gave you the note, leave word for me at the Wellington Road police station. In the meantime, here."

The boy looked at the silver Wyatt had put in his hand and whistled softly.

"Righty-ho, guv'ner. I'll keep my best eye out."

"Good for you."

They watched him go, then Andrew asked, "Is the note about Sara?"

"Yes," said Wyatt. He gave the note to Mrs. Wiggins, who took it with hands that were not quite steady.

"What does it say?" asked Verna.

Mrs. Wiggins, who had been reading it, swallowed and read it out loud:

" 'We got your daughter. Here's her hair ribbon to prove it.' "

"*Is* it her hair ribbon?" asked Wyatt.

"Yes. 'If you go to the police or try any tricks, you'll never see her again. But if you do as you're told, you'll get her back safe and sound. We want two hundred pounds. Get it, and we'll let you know how to get it to us in a day or so.' "

"What are you going to do?" Verna asked Wyatt.

"What would you do if I weren't in on the case?"

"Go to the bank and get the two hundred pounds."

"Fine. Take a bag with you and do that. Then, when you get back home here, take the money out and put it away somewhere. We'll give you the money to give them."

"Why should you do that?"

"Because what we'll give you will look good, but it will be queer—counterfeit money. We'll try to spot them when they pick it up, but if we can't, we'll have a second chance to trace them when they try to pass it."

"Clever."

"But isn't this all dangerous?" asked Mrs. Wiggins. "I mean, can't it be for Sara? The note said that if I went to the police . . ."

"But you didn't," said Wyatt. "And since Tucker and I came in the back way, they can't know that we were here already."

"Do you think they're watching the place?" asked Andrew.

"I think it's very likely. It's clear from everything they've done so far that they know what they're doing."

"It's too bad *we* couldn't have had someone outside to spot whoever they had watching the house. That might have given us a lead."

"It might," said Wyatt. "But I'm sure you know what the problem was. We had no assurance that a note would be delivered by hand rather than through the mail. And besides—" He broke off at a polite knock.

"Yes? Come in," said Verna.

The door opened, and a rather nondescript man in stained overalls and an old cap came in. It was not until Andrew saw the trowel in his pocket that he recognized the mason who had been on the scaffold across the street.

"Oh, hello, Dodson," said Wyatt. "Came in the back way, I hope?"

"Yes, Inspector."

"This is Constable Dodson, one of our very good men," said Wyatt. Then, turning back to him, "Well?"

"Was the note we're interested in delivered by a boy —small, ragged, with spikey hair?"

"Yes."

"Well, someone did follow him, watched to make sure he delivered the note, then left."

"Description?" said Tucker, his notebook out and pencil ready.

"A rather short, slight man, about five foot three. A thin face with dark hair and dark eyes set close together. He was wearing a dark suit with a kingsman around his neck instead of a collar or tie."

"Any other characteristics or anything else that might help identify him?"

"Yes. If you look at him quickly, he looks as if he's smiling. But if you look at him more closely, you see he's not. I've a feeling he's dangerous."

"Thank you, Dodson."

"May I ask you something?" asked Andrew.

Dodson glanced at Wyatt and when he nodded, said, "Yes?"

"You were on the scaffold across the street, weren't you?"

"Yes."

"Every time I looked at you, you were working and had your back to the house here. How could you have seen anyone who followed the boy?"

With a slight smile, Dodson produced a small hand

mirror, held it up so that Andrew could see how he had looked over his shoulder without turning around.

"Oh. Of course," said Andrew.

"Will you go to central records at the Yard," said Wyatt, "and see if you can find anything about him there?"

"Yes, Inspector."

"Some day," said Tucker, "we'll have photographs of everyone who's ever been convicted of a crime on file. Then, when you're trying to identify someone, you'll look through the file for his picture."

"Sir Francis Galton has come up with something even more interesting than that," said Wyatt.

"What's that, Inspector?"

"He's been studying the prints that our fingers leave when we touch anything, and he's proved conclusively that no two people have the same fingerprints. If he can get the department to adopt his system of analyzing and recording fingerprints, can you imagine what that would do for police work?"

"It would make our job a lot easier," said Dodson.

"Yes, it would. But in the meantime, we have to do things the old way. If you find anything in central records, let me know, Dodson."

Dodson said he would and left.

"Have you any questions, Mrs. Wiggins?" asked Wyatt. "Is there anything you'd like to ask me?"

"No, Inspector," said Mrs. Wiggins. "I don't understand everything that's been going on, everything you're doing, but . . . Do you still feel the way you did yesterday, that you'll be able to get Sara back safe and sound?"

"We've learned several things today," said Wyatt. "The most important of which is that we're dealing with some very cool and smart customers who know just what they're doing. And frankly, I'd much rather deal with someone like that than with someone who's frightened and might lose his head. So . . . Yes, I repeat what I said yesterday. We're going to do everything in our power to get Sara back, and we've more reason than ever to expect we'll be able to."

6

The Second Note

At about two-thirty the next afternoon, Andrew got off
a light green Brixton omnibus just before it crossed Westminster Bridge and turned left on the Embankment on
his way to Scotland Yard. There had been no further
word from Sara's kidnappers, and he knew that his
mother had suggested that he report to Wyatt, not because she thought it was a useful bit of information, but
because she could see what effect his anxiety was having
on Mrs. Wiggins, and she wanted to get him away, out
of the house.

Knowing this, he still went gladly because it gave him
something to do and because he hoped that Wyatt would
have something to say that would lessen his fears and
make him feel better about the situation. Because, with
every hour that passed, he became more anxious and
more depressed. Walking gloomily along, he was brought

up short by a barrier around an excavation in the street. As he paused there, watching the navvies at work with their picks and shovels, he was struck by the complexity that lay beneath the streets of London, for besides the Underground and the sewers, there was a bewildering tangle of water and gas pipes and conduits carrying telegraph lines.

Continuing around the edge of the excavation, he wondered how much of it would be left in, say, a thousand years, and what some Layard, Heinrich Schliemann or Flinders Petrie of the future would make of it. And thinking that, he thought again of what Wyatt had said about archeology and detective work.

He went in through the archway that was the main entrance to the Yard, crossed the courtyard and entered the building. He gave his name to the desk sergeant, who passed it on to a constable; and a few minutes later, he was led upstairs and along a corridor to a numbered door. He knocked, was told to come in, and then he was in Wyatt's bare office, which seemed even smaller than usual because Sergeant Tucker was there too, sitting against the wall and using a corner of Wyatt's desk to copy something from his notebook onto an official form.

"Hello, Andrew," said Wyatt. "Well?"

"Mother and Mrs. Wiggins are standing by at home," he said, "but so far there's no word. We haven't heard anything."

"Is that what you came here to tell me?"

"Well, yes. Mother thought you'd like to know and . . . Well, we—she, Mrs. Wiggins and I—wondered whether you'd heard anything, found out anything."

"No. Nothing."

"What about the small dark man who was watching to make sure that Harry delivered the note?"

"Dodson spent all of yesterday and most of today down in central records, but so far he hasn't been able to make an identification."

"I see."

"Don't look so disappointed," said Tucker. "A lot of police work calls for patience. As I said yesterday, maybe someday we'll have pictures of criminals we can go through, and that'll speed things up. But, at the moment, it's a slow business."

"All right," said Andrew. "But are you still hopeful about finding Sara?"

"Of course we are," said Wyatt firmly. "I know how difficult this is for all of you, but there are times when there's nothing you can do but wait for more facts, new developments, something that will give you the lead you need."

"In the meantime, there's all your other work that has to be done," said Tucker. He gave Wyatt the material he'd been copying from his notebook. "Here are my notes on the Farnum case."

"Thanks, Sergeant. I'll look at them later."

Tucker shook his head. "The commissioner wants a report this afternoon."

Wyatt looked at him, then at Andrew. "A slave driver, that's what he is. Will you excuse me, Andrew? I'm afraid . . ."

There was a knock, and Tucker opened the door. The constable who had brought Andrew up was standing there. He handed Tucker a note. Tucker glanced at it, raised an eyebrow and gave it to Wyatt.

"It's your mother, Andrew," said Wyatt, reading it.

"Here?"

"Yes. Show her up, Diggs," he said to the constable. Then, to Tucker, "Do you mind if Andrew waits till we find out why she came here?"

"No," said Tucker. "I don't mind."

"She must have gotten some word about Sara," said Andrew.

"So I suspect."

A few minutes later there was another light tap on the door; Tucker opened it, and Verna came in.

"Another note?" said Wyatt.

"Yes." She took it out of her handbag, gave it to him. "It came shortly after you left," she said to Andrew.

"What does it say?"

"It tells us what to do about the money. We're to put it in a bag and leave it in a dustbin in Regent's Park."

"Here, Sergeant," said Wyatt, giving the note to

Tucker. "You'd better read it and write down the details because you're going to cover the delivery." Then to Verna, "How did you come here?"

"The way you came to the house. I went out the back way, through the stable and the mews and took a hansom."

"I knew I could count on you to do just what you should."

"Do you think someone's watching the house?" asked Andrew.

"I think it's possible, but since they've no reason to think you've been in touch with the police, I suspect they'd only watch the front. You have the counterfeit money we gave you?"

"Yes."

"All right. Go back home the way you came, get the money and have Fred drive you to the park and leave the money at the place the note tells you to."

"Should Mrs. Wiggins come with me?"

"Yes. After all, the note was addressed to her. Have you any questions, Sergeant?"

"No, sir," said Tucker, giving the note back to Verna. "I'll have three men cover the pickup, one of them Dodson so he can keep an eye out for the yob we've been looking for, the one who watched young Harry drop off the first note."

"Good idea. What will they be, park attendents?"

"Something like that. And a soldier walking out with

a nursemaid—whatever I can lay on at short notice. Which means I'd better get cracking." Bowing to Verna, he hurried out.

"I'd better go too," said Verna. "Are you coming, Andrew?"

"Would you mind if he stayed here for a while?" asked Wyatt. "There's something I want to talk to him about."

Verna looked at him sharply, then nodded.

"All right. I'll see you later, Andrew. At home." And she left too.

Andrew looked closely at Wyatt.

"You're worried, aren't you?" he said.

"Yes, a bit."

"Because of this second note."

"No. I'm glad we got it. It's when you lose contact with a kidnapper or blackmailer that you have reason to be concerned. There's something else I'm worried about—or perhaps I should say that's been puzzling me— from the beginning. Has it occurred to you that there's something very odd about it?"

"The kidnapping?"

"Yes. Why, out of all the possible girls in London, did they take Sara? After all, her mother's just a house-keeper who doesn't earn very much and would, at first glance, have trouble raising even the two hundred pounds they're asking as ransom."

"That's true. But what if they knew about mother and how she feels about Sara? She said she'd pay the two hundred pounds right off, and she'd probably pay a good deal more than that to get her back safely."

"I think she would, too. But that's just the point. If they *didn't* know about your mother, why did they pick Sara as a mark when there are thousands of other girls who would be much more profitable targets? And if they *did* know about your mother, why didn't they ask for more than two hundred pounds—which you said yourself your mother would have been glad to pay?"

Andrew whistled softly. "I see what you mean. I had a feeling there was something strange about the whole thing, but I couldn't put my finger on what it was. Do you have any explanation for it?"

"Yes. At least, a possible one."

"What is it?"

"That Sara was kidnapped by mistake."

"By mistake?"

"Yes. Suppose that whoever took her didn't know her and kidnapped her instead of some other girl?"

"But who was that other girl?"

"That was what I wanted to talk to you about. She was kidnapped on her way home from dancing school. Did she have any special friend there?"

"I don't know. The only girl at dancing school whose name I remember her mentioning was one named Maria."

"Maria what?"

"I don't know."

"Well, Miss Fizdale will know." He got up. "Do you

want to go there with me?" And when Andrew looked at him without answering, "All right. Sometimes even I ask silly or unnecessary questions."

They went out and downstairs. As they passed the desk, the sergeant on duty called out to Wyatt and gave him an envelope that must have been delivered by hand, since there was no stamp on it.

"The Travellers Club," said Wyatt, glancing at the address on the back. "Must be from my father. Excuse me."

He opened the envelope, read the note it contained, then, his face expressionless, folded it and put it in his pocket.

"Is he all right?" asked Andrew.

"My father? Why shouldn't he be?"

"He seemed pretty upset the other day when he came to our house looking for you."

"Yes, he was. And still is. He's worried about my sister-in-law, Harriet, who's gone off some place, disappeared."

"Disappeared?"

"Yes."

"Is there any connection between that, her disappearing, and what's happened to Sara?"

"What?" Wyatt looked at him with surprise, then shook his head. "No. There's no connection."

He said it so flatly and with such finality that Andrew did not dare ask him how he knew.

They picked up a hansom on the Embankment, Wyatt gave the cabby the address of the school, and they were off, bobbing and swaying, over to Whitehall and then north and west. Wyatt was strangely quiet, and as they went up the Haymarket, he took his father's note out of his pocket and read it again. Then, catching Andrew's eye on him, he said, "I'm sorry. I'm afraid I'm not very good company at the moment."

"Well, this isn't exactly a tea fight. But can I ask you something?"

"Of course."

"Do you intend to tell Mrs. Wiggins and my mother what you told me—that you think Sara may have been kidnapped by mistake?"

"No. Your mother is an extremely intelligent woman and she may have a feeling, as you did, that there was something odd about it. But I think Mrs. Wiggins has been too upset for that to have occurred to her. In any case, I don't intend to tell either of them of my suspicions."

"Why?"

"Because, frightening as a kidnapping is, this is even more frightening. Ordinarily, a kidnapping is fairly straightforward. It's purpose is to get money, and when the money is paid, the kidnapped person is returned."

"Always?"

Wyatt looked at him and then away. "No, not always. That's why kidnapping is one of the most terrifying crimes we have to deal with. But if an ordinary kidnapping is a chancey matter, then you can see how what we're up against—a case where money isn't the real issue—is even more uncertain."

"But they did ask for money—two hundred pounds."

"I think they did that so it would *seem* like an ordinary kidnapping. Don't forget that they don't know—at least I hope they don't—that we, the police, are in on the case. If they ask for a reasonable ransom—which they've done—and tell Mrs. Wiggins not to get in touch with the police, there's a good chance that she won't. Not for a while, anyway. But if Sara disappears with no word from anyone, then her mother is bound to go to the police immediately. So what they've been doing is buying time."

Andrew nodded. "I see."

When the hansom drew up in front of the school, Wyatt told the cabby to wait. They could hear the pounding of the piano and the not entirely sylphlike sound of feet even before they crossed the garden to the front door, and the sounds continued even after Wyatt tugged on the bellpull. It was several minutes before the young maid opened the door, and when she did, it was clear from her expression that she recognized Wyatt.

"Good afternoon, sir," she said.

"I'd like to speak to Miss Fizdale, please."

"I'm afraid she's busy, sir. With the afternoon class."

"Do you know who I am?"

"Yes, sir. You were here the other day. You're the inspector from Scotland Yard."

"That's right. And now I'm here again, and I want to see Miss Fizdale again, so get her for me."

"Yes, sir."

Eyes on Wyatt and mouth slightly open, she backed up a few steps, then turned and hurried over to the large double doors of the parlor, knocked and went in. The piano broke off in the middle of a chord, the sound of shuffling feet stopped and after a moment Miss Fizdale came out, frowning slightly and with her lips compressed.

"Good afternoon, Inspector," she said coldly. "I assume there's some good reason for this interruption."

"I believe there is."

"You've found Sara Wiggins?"

"No. We're still looking for her. I'm here today to see another girl in her class, a friend of Sara's named Maria."

"Maria Milanovitch?"

"Is she the only Maria in the class?"

"Yes."

"Then I'd like to talk to her if I may."

"I'm afraid she's not here today."

"She's not?"

"No."

"Were you expecting her?"

"Yes. As a matter of fact, I was. She's usually very

regular in her attendance, especially lately, since I started doing special work with her at her mother's request."

"Was she here yesterday?"

"Yes, she was. Of course, she may be indisposed . . ."

"Do you know her home address?"

"Yes. It's Mornington Crescent. I'm not sure of the number, but . . . Just a second." She went back into the large front room, returned with a register bound in red morocco. She opened it, ran a finger down one of the pages and said, "It's number twelve Mornington Crescent."

"Thank you," said Wyatt, turning to leave.

"Excuse me, Inspector, but you're not going there—to her house, are you?"

"Why?"

"Because her mother, the countess, is a very anxious woman, and . . ."

"I'll do my best not to alarm her," said Wyatt. "Come on, Andrew." And he hurried across the garden to the waiting hansom. "Twelve Mornington Crescent," he told the cabby. "And hurry!"

7

The Missing Friend

With its two rubber-tired wheels, the hansom was easily the most maneuverable vehicle in London. And whether the cabby knew who Wyatt was or not, his manner was such that when he said hurry the cabby did. Turning the hansom sharply, he put his horse into a fast trot over toward Abbey Road, then south and east toward Regents Park.

"Did she say Milanovitch?" said Andrew.

"Yes."

"Sounds Middle European."

"Yes. Slavic. Sara never said anything about it, the fact that she was foreign?"

"No. Do you think that the countess may not speak English?"

"If she's been living here for any length of time, the

chances are she does. In any case, there's always French and German."

Andrew nodded. Cutting in front of a brougham, the hansom swung into Prince Albert Road, went east around the park and, driving through Park Village East, turned left and drew up in front of 12 Mornington Crescent. While not as theatrical as Nash's Park Crescent, Mornington Crescent had its own discreet elegance. Number 12 was a Georgian brick house with graceful iron railings in front of it. Again Wyatt told the cabby to wait, and he and Andrew went up the three low steps and rapped sharply with the polished brass knocker.

A butler opened the door almost at once.

"Is the countess in?" asked Wyatt.

"I will inquire," said the butler. "Who shall I say is calling?"

Wyatt gave him his card. The butler bowed, picked up a silver salver and tapping diffidently on the ornate door to the left of the hall, went in. A moment later he came out again.

"The countess will see you, sir," he said, holding the door open.

Wyatt and Andrew went in. The room was large and airy, and the Empire furniture made it seem light and feminine. The countess was sitting at a writing desk set against the far wall. Andrew was not quite certain what he expected, probably someone dark and Slavic, but the woman who turned and looked at them enquiringly was nothing like that. Wearing a lavender silk dress, she was fair and blue-eyed, and when she spoke, it was without a trace of an accent.

"Good afternoon, Inspector."

"Good afternoon, Countess." He hesitated. "You *are* the Countess Milanovitch?"

"Yes, I am," she said smiling.

"I was going to compliment you on your English, but . . . You *are* English, aren't you?"

"Born in Cheltenham," she said, nodding. "Many people find it puzzling or disconcerting."

"That a foreign countess speaks English so well?"

"Yes. But you solved the mystery very quickly. I was born and brought up here, met the count in Paris. We met again when he was posted to the embassy here, were married and have been living here ever since."

"Which embassy was he posted to?"

"The Serbian embassy. The count is the first secretary. Now perhaps you will introduce your young friend and also tell me what I can do for you."

"I'm sorry. This is Andrew Tillett. He's a friend of a friend of your daughter, Maria, and actually it is she we would like to talk to."

"Maria? This becomes more and more intriguing. I could not imagine why a police inspector should want to talk to me. But that you should want to talk to my daughter . . ."

"We're hoping that she can give us some information about her friend and Andrew's, Sara Wiggins."

"Sara Wiggins. Yes, I believe I remember Maria's mentioning her. Unfortunately she's not here now. She's at dancing school."

"Miss Fizdale's?"

"Why, yes."

"I'm afraid she isn't, Countess."

"What do you mean?"

"We've just come from there, and Miss Fizdale told us that she was not there today."

"But that's impossible," she said, frowning. Reaching up, she tugged at an embroidered bellpull. "Saunders," she said when the butler entered," did Burke take Miss Maria to dancing school this afternoon?"

"Yes, Countess. He did."

"Will you send him here, please?"

"Yes, Countess." He paused. "I did not wish to disturb you, but this just arrived." He presented the silver salver with an envelope on it.

"Oh?" She picked it up and looked at it. "Who brought it?"

"I cannot say. It was pushed through the letter slot. But it is marked urgent."

"Yes, I see that. Forgive me," she said to Wyatt and Andrew, and frowning, she opened the envelope. They watched her as she read the enclosure. She had been a little uneasy before, then somewhat irritated. But now,

reading the note on nondescript paper that looked familiar to them, the color drained from her face.

"Countess, what's wrong?" asked Wyatt.

"What?" She looked up at him as if she had forgotten
that he was there. "Nothing."

"That's not true. You're frightened. No, more than
frightened, terrified. What did that note say?"

"Nothing," she said again, her voice unsteady. She
got up. "I'm afraid I must ask you to forgive me. I . . ."

"Shall I tell you what it says? It says that whoever
wrote the note has your daughter, Maria. That if you
ever want to see her again, you must not go to the police
or communicate with them in any way. And—"

"No!" she said, her voice rising. "That's not true
either. It . . . it's a note from my husband. He wants me
to come to the embassy immediately. Excuse me!" and
she hurried from the room, the note crumpled in her
hand.

"She's lying, isn't she?" said Andrew.

"Yes," said Wyatt. "The note was on the same paper
as the one Mrs. Wiggins got."

"What does it mean?"

"That we're too late. She won't talk to us now. But it
confirms what I thought—what I told you before."

8

Maria

Sara pressed her ear to the door and listened. Something had been going on downstairs earlier; there had been a certain amount of talk and then someone or several people had left. But now all was quiet, and if her captors followed the previous day's pattern, no one would be coming up to the attic again until Sergeant Zerko brought supper. Satisfied, she crossed the room and took a glass from under the chest of drawers. The liquid in it had darkened even more since she had hidden it and had become a very satisfactory black.

Now that she was about to take the next step in her plan, what she was doing seemed so obvious that she found it difficult to remember how the idea had come to her. It had probably begun during her first night there in the attic. It was one thing to tell herself that she was Sara Wiggins, a smart and resourceful girl, and that she wasn't going to get dithery about what had happened to her. It was another to wake in the middle of the night and not know where she was or how she had gotten there. When she *did* remember, her heart skipped a beat and then began thudding, and she decided that while she didn't have to get dithery, perhaps she should do some thinking about the predicament she was in.

On the positive side, she was not only smart—as she kept telling herself she was—she was also lucky. How many girls were there in London who had Scotland Yard's best and most intelligent inspector as a friend? If anyone could find and rescue her, it would be he, especially with Andrew to help him—and Wyatt would be the first to admit that she, Sara, and Andrew had been a great help to him in previous cases.

That was quite a good deal to have on the positive side. On the other hand, London was very big, and both the lady with the red wig and Colonel Kosta seemed pretty smart too, so perhaps she's better see what she herself could do about getting out of the pickle she was in. (Besides, when she did get out—and one way or another of course she would—it would make a lot better story if she had done something to save herself instead of just waiting to be rescued.) So the next morning, as soon as it was light, she would go over the attic carefully and see if there was any way she could escape from it.

Her study of the attic was not particularly fruitful. The lock on the door was a good one and beyond her ability to pick, and the bars on the window were too sturdy to be removed by anything less than a hacksaw or a file. The only thing she came across that might be of use was a loose nail that she pulled out of the window-sill. And it *was* of use. For when she discovered that there was no way that she could escape, she decided that the next best thing would be to get a message out. The question then was what to write it on. There was little point in asking for pen and paper; her captors would not be foolish enough to give it to her. But they might give her something to read—and if they did, she had an idea of what she could do about it.

So when the sergeant brought up her breakfast, she told him she wanted to talk to the colonel; and when *he* finally came up, she told him she was going loopy not having anything to do and couldn't she at least have something to read? He must have consulted the biddy with the red wig because *she* came up about a half-hour later and said the only book they had around was a Bible and how was that? Sara made a face and said she'd rather have something else, but after all there were stories in the Bible, so that was all right. The red-wigged lady watched her while they talked, seemed satisfied, and gave her the Bible and left.

Actually Sara was delighted, not just because there *was* a good deal of reading in the Bible, but for other reasons as well. Hoping that anyone who heard about it would understand her problem and forgive her, she pulled off the back cover of the Bible, tore it into small pieces and put them in a glass of water to steep. Then, with the sharp point of the nail she had salvaged, she cut out the blank page that was just inside the back cover.

In the twenty four hours since she had started steeping the fragments of the cover, the black dye had darkened the water nicely. Now, using it as ink and the nail as a stylus, she wrote the following note:

Help! My name is Sara Wiggins and I am being held a prisoner somewhere near here. Give this message to a constable and tell him to notify Inspector Peter Wyatt of Scotland Yard who is my friend and will find me. This is not a joke or a cod. It's the truth. Please, please help me!

Sara Wiggins

Though not quite as dark as regular ink, the writing was completely legible, and Sara was quite pleased with it. Taking the cake of soap from the dish on the washstand, Sara wrapped the note around it and tied it with a strip torn from the edge of her petticoat.

She walked to the barred window that faced west and stood there for a moment looking out at the small section of street that she could see there. Ideally, that's where she would have liked to drop the note—on that fairly wide and busy street—but the intervening roof made that difficult. She would have to throw the soap-weighted note fairly high in order to clear it, and, if she threw it too high and too hard it would land on the roofs on the other side of the street, while if she didn't throw it hard enough, it would fall short and land on the roof on her side.

Shrugging, she went to one of the southern dormer windows and looked out. There was no one in sight. Leaning out, she threw the cake of soap and the note that enclosed it as far to the right as she could. It landed very close to where she had hoped it would; about half-way to the corner and close to the center of the cobbled alley, where anyone who came through would be sure to see it.

She was standing there, wondering how long it would be before someone picked it up, when she heard the outside door open and close. There was a brief exchange—she thought she recognized the colonel's voice and that of the woman with the red wig—then heavy footsteps started up the stairs. She hurried over to the cot and sat down. The footsteps drew closer and stopped outside the door. A key rattled, the door was unlocked and opened. Colonel Kosta and the woman with the red wig came in, followed by Sergeant Zerko. He was carrying a girl of about Sara's age whose eyes were closed and who was breathing heavily. Sara stared, watching as he put her down on the cot next to hers. Then, as he stood up and Sara could see the girl's face, she said, "Maria!"

The woman with the red wig looked at her sharply.

"You know this girl?" she asked.

"Yes."

"What's her name?"

"Maria."

"Maria what?"

"Milanovitch."

Smiling a little, the woman with the red wig glanced at the colonel, and he nodded.

"All right," he said. "I'm satisfied." He turned to Sara. "She's asleep the way you were when we brought you here. Take care of her when she wakes up and tell her that she has nothing to worry about. And neither have you."

"You mean you're going to let us go?"

"Yes."

"When?"

"Soon. In a few days."

Sara looked hard at him, then at the woman with the red wig. Her face was expressionless, as the colonel's was, but somehow Sara knew that he was lying. They had no intention of freeing them, but there was no point in letting them know that she knew that.

"All right," she said. She went over to the other cot, and as she bent over Maria, she heard her three captors leave. Maria's eyes were closed and her breath was not only shallow but had the sickeningly sweet odor that Sara had smelled when that wet pad had been clamped to her nose.

"Maria," she said. "Wake up!"

Maria did not move. Going over to the washstand, Sara soaked her towel in the pitcher, wrung it out and wiped Maria's face with it. Maria moaned faintly, and when Sara placed the damp cloth on her forehead, she opened her eyes slowly, looked at Sara and said, "Sara."

"That's right. How do you feel?"

"Sick." She looked around the attic. "What is this place? How did I get here?"

"Don't you remember?"

"No. At least . . . I was going to dancing school. Burke took me in the victoria. A cart and four-wheeler were blocking the street, so I said I'd get out and walk. Burke didn't want me to, but I was late and I insisted, so he let me out and drove off. As I went past the four-wheeler, the driver called to me. When I went over to see what he wanted, he grabbed me and . . ." She had been talking more and more slowly as it came back to her. Now her eyes dilated. "I've been kidnapped!"

"Yes."

"Merciful heavens, you too?"

"Yes."

"Are they . . . are they white slavers?"

"I don't think so."

"But they must be! Otherwise why should they have kidnapped both of us? I mean, we're both young and pretty . . ."

"A little too young, don't you think?"

"No. They like them that way. Young and untouched —you know what I mean."

"Yes. How do you know so much about white slavers?"

"Our chambermaid had a book about them—about a girl who was kidnapped by them and what happened to her."

"I see. Well, I'm sorry to disappoint you, but I'm pretty sure they're not white slavers, not going to ship us off to China or Arabia."

"But then what do they want? Why did they kidnap two of us?"

"That's what I've been asking myself. When I first came to, a man they call the colonel asked me some questions and then got very angry, and it suddenly dawned on me that I wasn't the girl he thought I was. That I'd been kidnapped by mistake. I couldn't understand why or how, but now I do. They kidnapped me because they thought I was you."

"Why did they think that?"

"Do you remember what happened the day before yesterday?"

"No."

"We had finished class, put on our regular shoes and were just leaving when Miss Fizdale called you back and said your mother wanted you to work with her on something special."

"A court curtsey, so I'd be able to do one when I was presented to the king."

"What king?"

"King Alexander of Serbia."

"Oh. Anyway you said you weren't sure your coachman knew about it and you asked me to tell him to come back later."

"Yes, I remember that."

"Well, what I think happened is that Sergeant Zerko, the big, bearded man who kidnapped me, didn't know me, but he knew your carriage. Don't you have a coat of arms or something like that on the door?"

"Yes. The Serbian eagle."

"Well, he saw me talk to your coachman and then go off, and he thought I was you, so he followed me and kidnapped me. And when they discovered that they'd made a mistake, they tried again, and this time they did get you."

"But why do they want me? If they're not white slavers, is it for money, ransom?"

"Maybe. Is your father rich?"

"Yes. He's the king's cousin. And mother's family is rich too, and they all love me very much and would pay anything to get me back again."

"Well, then you've got nothing to worry about—I don't think."

It was some time after this that there was a knock on the door of Mrs. Wiggins's room. She was no longer crying—she had finally gotten hold of herself—but she was still clutching her damp handkerchief, and she touched her eyes with it and put it in her pocket before she said, "Come in." Then, as the door opened. "Oh, it's you, ma'am." She looked at Verna hopefully. "Have you heard anything? Is there any word?"

"No. I just thought I'd see how you were."

"I'm all right."

"Are you? Then why didn't you eat any supper? Annie said she brought you a tray, but you didn't touch anything on it."

"I'm sorry. I'm afraid I'm just not hungry."

"Why are you sorry?"

"I just am."

"Well, that's one thing we won't put up with. You can be angry, bitter, worried, almost anything you like, but not sorry."

"I can't help it—I *am* sorry. Not just for all the trouble I'm causing you . . ."

"Is it you who's causing the trouble?"

"No. But you know what I mean. Besides, I'm supposed to be taking care of things here, the house and all that, and these last few days, ever since Sara disappeared . . ."

"You've been acting like a mother and not a housekeeper, and no one here would have you act any other way."

"You're being awfully nice about it, Miss Tillett, just as you've always been about everything, and that only makes it worse because . . ." She broke off, her eyes filling with tears again. "What do you think is going to happen? Do you think we'll ever get her back again?"

"Of course we will. I don't have to tell you how Inspector Wyatt feels about Sara. I think she means almost as much to him as she does to the rest of us. And ever since we got that ransom note, he's felt very optimistic about locating whoever it is that's got her."

"Yes, I know. It's just that it's three days now, and it's . . ."

"Difficult."

"Yes." Mrs. Wiggins dabbed at her eyes again, then forced a faint smile. "Well, you've made me feel a little better, just as you always do."

"If that's true, will you do something for me?"

"Of course. Anything."

"Then let me have Annie bring back your tray, and you try to eat a little something."

"All right. I'll try."

"Good. You're a real trouper." She embraced the

housekeeper, kissed her quickly and went out.

Andrew, who had come up with her and was waiting at the top of the stairs, looked at her questioningly.

"She's very worried, upset, but she agreed to try to eat something." Then, as he nodded approvingly, "You said the inspector feels that this new development, the fact that another girl has been kidnapped, could give him an important lead."

"Yes. I'm not sure he knows exactly what it means yet, but I do know he considers that—and the chance that his men saw who picked up the money you left in the park—are the two most important developments in the case so far."

"I told you I looked around when Mrs. Wiggins put the bag in the dustbin, but I didn't see anyone who looked even remotely like a policeman."

"If they were as good as they're supposed to be, you wouldn't."

"When will we know if anything came of it?"

"The inspector must know already. I'll know tomorrow."

"You're going down to the Yard again?"

"Yes. He told me to come down first thing in the morning. He thinks I might be useful."

Sara was more than half asleep when she heard the muffled sound from the other cot. She sat up, peering through the darkness, and even though she couldn't see, she knew what it was; Maria weeping with her face buried in the pillow.

"Maria?"

"Yes."

"What is it?"

"I'm frightened."

"Why?"

"I just am. I don't like this place. I don't like that woman with the red hair or the man who was with her or what they gave us for supper and . . . Well, I'm frightened, that's all."

"I don't blame you for not liking the woman. I think her name's Addie, and I don't think it's her own hair. I think it's a wig. And I don't blame you for not liking Sam or the food or this place, but there's no reason to be frightened."

"Why not? You said they're not white slavers and maybe they're not. But if they're not, we don't know who they are or what they want. And if it's not just money or even if it is . . . Well, how do we know that they'll let us go?"

"Oh, I think they will. You said your father would pay anything to get you back, didn't you?"

"Yes. But . . ."

"I know. You're wondering how we know they'll keep their word. We don't—and I'm not counting on it—

but I still say we've got nothing to worry about. Shall I tell you why?"

"Yes. Please."

"I don't think anyone's listening, but I'd better whisper it anyway." She knelt down next to Maria's cot, put her mouth next to her ear. "Did you ever heard of Peter Wyatt?"

"No."

"He's the smartest, bravest and best inspector in Scotland Yard, and he's a very good friend of mine. And the minute my mother and my friend Andrew discovered I was gone, I'm sure they got in touch with him. And if they did, and he and Sergeant Tucker are looking for us, then you can be certain that they'll find us and rescue us very soon, within the next day or so."

"Both of us? Me too?"

"Of course, you too. But that's not all. Just before they brought you in here, I wrote a note on a page I tore out of the back of a Bible with ink I made and a nail as a pen, and I threw it out of the window."

"What did you say in it?"

"I said who I was and asked anyone who found it to give it to a constable. The constable will get it to Inspector Wyatt at the Yard, and that'll be that. The inspector will be here in two twos!"

"Oh. I never did know you very well, Sara, but I always liked you even though I was a little jealous of the way you could dance. But now . . . Well, if I had to be kidnapped, I can't think of anyone I'd rather be kidnapped with than you."

"Well, with everything I've done and everything I know," said Sara seriously," I really don't think you could do better."

At about that same time a stooping, gray-bearded rag and bone man with a foul-smelling gunnysack slung over his shoulder turned into the alley that was under the attic's south windows. He stepped on something, swore, picked it up and went back to the nearest gas light to examine it. It turned out to be a cake of soap wrapped in some fairly stiff paper. There was some writing on the paper but since he couldn't read, it meant nothing to him. Putting the soap away in an inside pocket of his torn jacket, he crumpled up the paper and dropped it into the gutter where the night wind played with it, blowing it here and there, but always down the street, until it finally blew it into the Thames.

9

The Royal Visit

When Andrew arrived at Wyatt's office the following morning, the inspector was out and Sergeant Tucker was sitting at the desk going through some folders.

"He'll be back in a minute," he told Andrew. "Sit down."

"Thanks. What happened yesterday?"

"Where?"

"At Regent's Park. Didn't you have some men there watching to see who picked up the ransom money?"

"Oh, that. Yes. It was the same nipper who brought the note to your house."

"Harry, the bootblack?"

"Yes."

"Well, that's good, isn't it?"

"Why good?"

"Well, he's a bright boy, and he said he'd help us."

"What he said and what he'll do—be able to do—could be two very different things."

"You don't think that this time he'll make a point of getting a look at the man who sent him to pick up the money?"

"If the yobs we're dealing with are at all sharp, they won't give him a chance to. We sent Dodson over to the Wellington Road police station to see if he left any word there for us as we asked him to."

"Anything else new?"

"On Sara? No. I'm going over his nibs's other cases to see if I can keep them from boiling over while he works on this one."

Wyatt came in, nodded to Andrew. "Any word from Dodson?" he asked Tucker.

"No. Give him time. He doesn't gad about London in hansoms like some people I know. A bus is good enough for him."

"Well, it's not for me when I'm in a hurry. I'm going over to the Foreign Office. He'd better be here when I get back. I have an appointment to talk to Chadwick senior," he said to Andrew. "Want to come with me?"

"Yes." Then, as they went down the stairs, "Why the Foreign Office?"

"Do you remember who Maria's father is?"

"First Secretary of the Serbian Embassy."

"Right. I want to talk to him, but before I do, I thought I should speak to someone who can brief me on a few things. For instance, what do you know about Serbia?"

"Well, I know it's one of the Balkan countries. I think it's just south of Hungary."

"It is. And surrounded by more other countries than you can shake a stick at. What else?"

"Don't they have a new and very young king?"

"Yes. Alexander. He's just sixteen. But why did you call it the *Serbian* Embassy?"

"Because that's what the countess called it. I always thought the country was called Servia."

"So did I. It's what it's called in the atlas. I'd like to know which is correct, and I'd also like to know whether Alexander is or isn't coming here."

"Is he supposed to be coming?"

"He was until a few days ago, but there was no mention of it in the press either yesterday or today."

"I see. And do you think this has something to do with Sara's disappearance?"

"Well, it may have something to do with her friend Maria's disappearance—and we agreed that that had something to do with Sara."

"True."

They went out the rear of the Yard and to Parliament Street by way of the Derby Gate. Andrew thought they would be going into the building by way of the Downing Street entrance, but crossing Parliament Street, Wyatt opened a small and inconspicuous door between the Home and Foreign Offices and went in. The uniformed commissionaire behind the desk apparently knew and was expecting him, for he bowed and said something to a young man in a very elegant morning coat who was standing by.

"Inspector Wyatt?" asked the young man approaching him.

"Yes."

"My name's Wyndham. Mr. Chadwick asked me to bring you up to his office. This way." And he led them along labyrinthine corridors, up an ornate staircase and along another corridor to a heavy, dark door. He knocked, opened the door and stood back so that Wyatt and Andrew could enter, then followed them in.

The room was large and handsome. There was a desk and several chairs in it, but Chadwick was not sitting at the desk. He was standing at the window and looking out at the ducks in the St. James Park lake.

"Good morning," he said to Wyatt. "And good morning to you too, Andrew. Though I must confess I'm a little surprised to see you. I assumed from your note," he said to Wyatt, "that what you wanted to talk to me about was a police matter."

"It is."

"I remember now that my son said that Andrew had been involved in several of your cases."

"He was not just involved. He was very helpful."

"I congratulate him. And you too. Now what can I do for you?"

"We're going over to see someone at the Servian Embassy this afternoon and, before we go, there are a few things I would like to ask you about."

"It's a country I'm particularly interested in, know a good deal about, and I'll be glad to tell you anything you want to know. To begin with, don't call it Servia. Call it Serbia."

"I wondered about that. The atlas calls it Servia."

"I know. I don't know where that originated, but the Serbs resent it bitterly. They claim we're the only people in Europe who call it that—which is true—and that we do it because we believe the name derives from *servus*, meaning slave."

"I see. I'll be careful about it."

"Do. Would you care to tell me what you're going to see about?" Then, as Wyatt hesitated, "Quite all right if you'd rather not talk about it. I just wondered if this was related to something I asked you about when we met at Lord's."

"Whether the Yard ever operated outside the country."

"Yes. I told you that there'd been a shooting at our Embassy in Paris. What I didn't tell you was that the man who was shot was the Serbian ambassador to France."

Wyatt's eyebrows went up. "That's interesting. Has the murderer been caught?"

"Though the ambassador was badly wounded, fortunately he did not die and will recover. As to who did the shooting—or at least is responsible for it—anyone who knows anything about Serbia, its history and present status, could probably guess."

"That of course is one of the reasons we came to see you—to learn something about our relations with Serbia."

"I would say that they are not only warm and friendly, but protective. And for a very good reason. If there is going to be a major war—and there are many who feel that it is inevitable—it will undoubtedly start in the Balkans."

"The powder keg of Europe."

"Exactly. And if that's true, then Serbia could well be the fuse—especially since young Alexander became king."

"That happened recently, didn't it?"

"About four months ago. Before that, ever since the late king's death, Serbia was ruled by a regent, General Petroff. The reason the situation there is so unstable is that the general was not only reluctant to give up his power, but his bid for power was backed by several other countries that are not particularly friendly to us. The Serbian people, on the other hand, hated the general and love young Alexander—which is one of the reasons we support him, and which, in turn, is why he is coming here."

"He *is* coming?"

"Yes. Either tomorrow or the next day. You didn't know about it?"

"No. There was some mention of it in the press, and then it was dropped."

"There's been a certain amount of conflict about it between us here in the Foreign Office and your Special Branch, which is responsible for protecting the king. They would like to keep the whole thing as quiet as possible, whereas we want the whole country to know about it. The controversy has finally been settled in our favor, and since you seem particularly interested in Serbia, I think you should be apprised of the Special Branch's plans."

"That might be helpful," said Wyatt.

"Good. Percy," he said to his young assistant, "would you talk to Sir Roger and arrange it?"

"Of course," said Wyndham and left the room.

"Now is there anything else I can tell you?"

"I'm not sure," said Wyatt. "I assume General Petroff was responsible for the shooting of the ambassador."

"I don't think there's any doubt about it. He's been plotting against the king ever since he had to give up the regency. He probably tried to get the ambassador to join him and, when he refused, had him shot."

"I see. Is there anything else you think I should know?"

"Well, I've prepared some background material you

might want to look at, especially if you're going to be talking to Sir Roger."

He took some papers from a portfolio on his desk and gave them to Wyatt. As Wyatt sat down and began going through them, Andrew went to one of the windows and looked out. To his left, through the huge elms that shaded this portion of the park, he could see the suspension bridge that crossed the lake. The last time he was in London, he and Sara had stood there, near the middle of the bridge, trying to identify the varieties of ducks and geese that were swimming there and watching the pelicans at the Horse Guards end of the lake through a pair of his mother's opera glasses. Where was Sara now? Was she thinking of him as he was of her?

There must have been something in Andrew's expression that attracted Chadwick's attention and either piqued his interest or prodded his memory, for he now asked, "How's your friend?"

"Friend?"

"The girl who was at Lord's with you—Sara Wiggins?"

As Andrew hesitated, Wyatt looked up from the papers he was reading.

"She's fine," he said firmly and unequivocally. Then, indicating the papers, "These are very interesting. May I take them along with me?"

"Of course. They're copies I had made for the Special Branch."

"Thank you very much for that and for your briefing. It's been very helpful."

"I'm glad. Because I have a feeling that you're going to be very helpful to us in this particular matter."

"I hope you're right."

Chadwick nodded to them, and they left.

"I'm sorry I didn't answer when he asked about Sara," said Andrew.

"You're not as used to the unexpected question as I am. Besides, I meant what I said."

"You really do think she's all right?"

"Yes, I do."

Without a guide, they lost their way in the winding and confusing corridors, and so it took considerably longer to get back to Scotland Yard than it had to get to see Chadwick. Deep in thought, Wyatt pushed open the door of his office, then paused. Sergeant Tucker was still at Wyatt's desk, but he was not alone. Sitting in the straight-backed chair in the corner, hands resting on the crook of a tightly furled umbrella, was General Wyatt.

"Oh, good morning, sir. Have you been here long?"

"No. Just a few minutes. I hope you don't mind my stopping by, but I haven't heard from you in several days and I wondered if you had any word for me."

"No, sir. I'm afraid I haven't."

"Oh," said the general, trying to conceal his disappointment. "Do you have any idea when you might have?"

"No, sir. But if you'll give me just a minute, we can talk about it." He turned to Tucker. "Anything for me, Sergeant?"

"Yes, Inspector. A telegram from the Bristol police." He gave it to him. "They caught Keefe, dressed as an American minister, as he was about to board a steamer for the States."

"Smart work," said Wyatt, reading the telegram. "Anything else?"

"Dodson's back. There was no word from the boot-black at the Wellington Road police station."

"That's strange. Tell him to go look for the boy. If he's not at the Underground station, maybe one of the other boys knows where he is. But I want him found."

"I already sent him off to do that."

"Good. Anything else?"

"No, Inspector."

"Then, sir," said Wyatt to his father, "I'm at your service. Would you like to—" He broke off at a knock. "Damnation! Yes?"

The door opened, and Wyndham came in.

"So you're back, Inspector," he said. "I was afraid I might have to leave a message for you. Sir Roger sends his compliments and would like you to accompany him to a meeting of the Special Branch."

"Now?"

"Yes. I was to bring you if you were here."

"I see. I'm sorry, sir," he said to the general.

"Is that Sir Roger Brandon, the Foreign Secretary?"

"Yes, it is."

"Well," the general forced a smile, "I think his needs should take precedence over mine. Run along."

"Thank you, sir. I'll get back to you in a day or so. Why don't you stay and have lunch with the sergeant?" he said to Andrew. "Then, if I'm through in time, we can take care of our little matter."

"Right."

Wyndham opened the door, and with a final, apologetic glance at his father, Wyatt followed him out.

"He seems rather busy," said the general.

"That he is, sir," said Tucker. "And there's good reason for it. There's not a keener, more highly regarded inspector in the Yard."

"Is that so?"

"Yes, it is. Take this telegram we just got. For almost a year now we've been looking for a very clever counterfeiter. A few weeks ago they asked the inspector to take over the case. He not only discovered who the man was— a chap named Keefe—but when he disappeared, he told them to watch the ports, that he'd try to leave the country disguised as a minister. Which is just what he did."

"That is rather amazing. I feel guilty about troubling him with my affairs, which are not of empire-shaking importance."

"Anything that concerns you would be of great importance to him, General," said Andrew. "I know that he has the highest regard for you, and I'm certain that he'll solve your problem, whatever it is."

"You think so? I hope you're right. But, in the meantime, I thank you for your words of encouragement."

10

The Embassy

The Serbian Embassy was on Claverton Street, just a short distance north of Gloucester Road and the river, but Andrew and Wyatt didn't get there until late in the afternoon. As soon as the general left, Sergeant Tucker took Andrew to lunch at a pub on the corner of Whitehall Street, which was apparently a great favorite with the men of the Yard. It seemed that the sergeant had a passion for Scotch eggs, and unbelievable as it might seem to someone with an average appetite and normal digestion, he ate three of them along with a beef sandwich.

While Andrew ate his sandwich, Tucker held forth on one of his favorite subjects: the general excellence of Wyatt's character and his brilliance as a detective. It had been obvious to Andrew that Tucker admired Wyatt; and since he shared that admiration, he enjoyed listening to the sergeant's encomiums. Though aware of Wyatt's social background and education, Tucker was not at all impressed with them and seemed to think that the inspector was an outstanding police officer in spite of these rather than because of them. He felt that Wyatt's greatest qualification, besides his native intelligence, was the fact that he had walked the streets of London as an ordinary constable and therefore knew the city, its geography, structure and moods, as only a bobby can.

"But smart as he is," he said as they walked back to the Yard," he's still fairly young, and it would never do to let him know how I feel about him. That's why I give him the needle about things like being impatient and forever riding in hansoms like a toff." At this point, suddenly remembering why Andrew was there, he said, "I know this is hard for you, but don't *you* start getting impatient now. We're as anxious to find Sara as you are, and find her we will!"

It was after three when Wyatt returned to the office, explaining that the meeting with Sir Roger and the Special Branch had been a long one. After ascertaining that there had been no further word from Dodson and that nothing else required his immediate attention, he and Andrew left, taking a hansom to Claverton Street.

The embassy was an imposing stone building with a black iron railing around it. Wyatt told the cabby to wait, and he and Andrew walked up the steps past an arrogant cat that stared at them as if questioning their right to exist, let alone be there. Wyatt used the brass door knocker, and the door was opened by a porter wearing a livery coat, red waistcoat and knee breeches. Wyatt asked for the first secretary and, when he was told that he was not there, presented his card and insisted on seeing the next ranking official. The porter left, somewhat reluctantly, and a few minutes later returned with a slim and rather effete man in his middle thirties. He wore the virtually required diplomatic uniform of frockcoat, grey waistcoat and striped trousers, but there was something a little outré about them, as if he were determined to give them his own continental stamp: the shoulders of his coat were too padded and square, his trousers too narrow and the carnation in his buttonhole too large.

"I am Count Gradowsky," he said with a slight Slavic accent. "You wanted to see me?"

"Actually, we wanted to see Count Milanovitch," said Wyatt.

"Ah, yes. Unfortunately, he is not here. He has gone to Scotland."

"To Scotland?"

"Yes. Am I incorrectly pronouncing it? Should it be Scotchland or Scottishland?"

"No, no. Scotland's correct. It's just that I'm rather surprised. Why on earth did he go up to Scotland?"

"My dear inspector, I would not dream of asking him. After all, he is my senior, the first secretary. I am only the second secretary."

"Of course. But what puzzles me is not only why he should have gone there, but why he should have gone there *now*. Aren't you expecting your king?"

"Yes, our young king Alexander, long may he reign. He is coming tomorrow."

"And he'll be staying here, at the embassy?"

"Yes. The ambassador's quarters have been prepared for him."

"Where is the ambassador?"

"There is no ambassador. He was recalled when the regency ended and Alexander became king. Milanovitch, who had been first secretary, became chargé d'affaires, and he will probably be appointed ambassador when His Majesty arrives."

"Which makes it all the more surprising that he should have left now. Who will be responsible for making all the diplomatic and social arrangements for the king?"

"Most of that has already been done by Milanovitch and your Foreign Office. I am to see someone—Sir Roger Brandon?—about this tomorrow. And of course safety arrangements are in the hands of your Special Branch."

"Yes, I know. I was just at a meeting with Sir Roger and the people from the Special Branch."

"Then there is no reason to be puzzled or concerned, is it not true? In spite of Milanovitch's absence—and is it not possible that he is on a mission for the king?—all will be well and secure."

"I sincerely hope so. Well, thank you very much, Count."

"Not at all, Inspector. It has been a pleasure to meet you."

He bowed, snapped his fingers to summon the porter and remained standing there while the porter opened the door and showed them out.

"Well?" said Wyatt as they went down the steps.

"In spite of what he said, I think there's something strange about it," said Andrew. "Why would Milanovitch go away now, just when the king is coming?"

"Exactly what I was wondering, and of course did ask about. Though there is the possibility that the trip to Scotland—if that's where he went—concerns, not the king, but Maria."

"That's something *I* wondered about. Of course, Gradowsky never mentioned Maria . . ."

"He might not know about her. That she's gone, I mean. I think that's something we should look into."

The arrogant cat was gone, but the hansom was waiting. Wyatt gave the cabby the Milanovitch address on Mornington Crescent, and they went bowling off, going north on Denbigh Street.

"You're very quiet," said Wyatt as they went past Victoria Station on their way to Picadilly.

"Sorry. I was thinking."

"About what?"

"Several things. Your sister-in-law, for instance. You said there was no connection between her disappearance and Sara's."

"That's right."

"For some reason you don't seem terribly worried about finding her."

"I'm not."

"If you aren't, it's not because you don't care about her, because you do care. Which means . . . Do you know where she is?"

Wyatt looked at him sharply, then smiled.

"I keep forgetting that you see further through a brick wall than most people. Let's say, I think I may know."

"In other words, you think you'll be able to find her."

"Yes."

"What about Sara?"

Wyatt looked at him again, this time without smiling.

"That, my young friend, is a trick I have often used myself, but haven't often had used against me. You wanted to compare my response to your question about my sister-in-law to the one about Sara. What did you find out?"

"That you're not quite as sure about finding Sara as you are of finding your sister-in-law."

"True. But I'm just as determined to do so, perhaps even more so."

"Yes, I think you are."

"Then be patient, Andrew. I know this is very difficult for you, but there's a rhythm in cases as there is in most things. So far everything that's happened has been negative, but that's bound to change very soon."

"I hope you're right."

When they drew up in front of the house on Mornington Crescent, Wyatt again told the cabby to wait, led the way to the door and rapped with the knocker. When the butler opened the door, this time Wyatt did not ask if the countess was in. He said, "I'd like to see the countess."

"I'm afraid, Inspector, that that's impossible. The countess is indisposed."

"I'm sorry to hear that, but I'd still like to see her."

The butler studied him for a moment, then bowed. He let them into the entrance hall, tapped on the closed door of the drawing room, went in and, a moment later, came out again and, without saying anything further, held the door open.

The countess, wearing a dressing gown, was lying on a chaise longue. She was not just pale; she seemed to have aged in the short time since they had last seen her.

"Good afternoon, Countess," said Wyatt. "I'm sorry to hear that you haven't been well." Her gesture indicated that it was of no consequence. "I wondered if you'd had any further word about your daughter."

"I don't know what you mean," she said in a husky voice.

"When we came here to see her yesterday, you said she was at dancing school. We knew that she wasn't, that she hadn't been there, because we had just come from there. Then a note came that frightened you terribly. I'm certain it concerned Maria, but you insisted that it was from your husband at the embassy."

"Well?"

"We were just over at the embassy. I wanted to talk to the count because I thought he would listen to what I had to say with less emotion than you, but I was told that he was not there. That he had gone up to Scotland."

"That's correct. He went up there last night."

"Why?"

"Because . . . he had business to take care of up there."

"Business? He's chargé d'affaires at the embassy here, and tomorrow his king is arriving for his first state visit to England. What business could he have that is more important than that?"

"But the business he went to Scotland to take care of was the king's business—it was for the king."

"It did not concern your daughter?"

"Of course not. How could it concern her?"

"Then where is she?"

"She . . . she went with him—up to Scotland."

"I see."

He looked at her steadily, thoughtfully, until she colored faintly and said, "Why are you staring at me that way?"

"I'm sorry. I didn't mean to stare. I was just wondering how I could appeal to you, say what I want to say. I am convinced, Countess, that your daughter Maria has been kidnapped as her friend Sara was. If you will admit it, trust me and tell me what the kidnappers have told you to do, it could help us to find both girls. If you refuse to trust me, continue to insist that nothing is wrong, you will not only endanger both their lives, but much, much more than that."

"I tell you there is nothing wrong—absolutely nothing! Now will you please go?"

"Countess . . ."

"Please, please go!"

Her voice had risen, and it was clear that she was on the verge of hysteria.

"Of course," said Wyatt quietly. He bowed, and he and Andrew left.

"Well," he said when they were outside, "there's still no change. We didn't do any better here than we did at the embassy." Then, as the cabby pushed the lever that opened the hansom's low door, "Get in and I'll take you home."

They were silent during the short drive to Rysdale

Road. As the hansom drew up under the porte-cochere, the door opened and Matson came out.

"Good afternoon, Inspector," he said. "Miss Tillett was hoping you'd be stopping by with Master Andrew. She has a message for you."

"Oh, thank you, Matson."

Like Matson, Verna must have heard the hansom, for when Andrew and Wyatt went in, she was waiting for them.

"Dodson was here about a half-hour ago," she said. "He was going back to the Yard, but, on the chance that you might stop off here, he left a message for you here, too."

"Very foresighted of him," said Wyatt, taking the envelope she held out to him and opening it.

Verna looked at Andrew. She didn't say anything but her look asked if there was anything new. He shook his head.

"Well," said Wyatt, in a curiously flat voice, "this is interesting. He found Harry the bootblack."

"But that's good, isn't it?" asked Verna. "I mean, if it was he who picked up the money . . ."

"Yes. Under other circumstances it certainly would be good. But Dodson found him at St. Mary's Hospital."

"Was he hurt?" asked Andrew, knowing the answer from Wyatt's expression and tone of voice.

"You could call it that," said Wyatt grimly. "He had been stabbed, was unconscious and it's doubtful that he'll live. Whoever sent him to pick up the money apparently wanted to be sure that he wouldn't be able to make an identification."

Wyatt had talked about a rhythm in cases, claiming that things were bound to change for the better. Well, this was no change but just more of the same bad news.

Sara had been gone for four days now, and they had no more of a clue to her whereabouts than they had had in the beginning.

11

The Tosher

That night Andrew dreamed about Sara. There was nothing surprising about that; she was, after all, on his mind most of the time. In fact, whenever he wasn't thinking specifically about something else, he found himself thinking about her, worrying and feeling anxious about her. What was surprising was the form that the dream took and the effect it had on him.

He dreamed that he awoke and, lying there in bed, heard someone speaking. The voice was familiar but, for a moment, he couldn't place it until . . . Of course. It was Sara's voice!

"Sara?" he called, sitting up in bed.

"Yes."

"Where are you?"

"Here."

"Where's here?"

"Here!" she said with a touch of annoyance, then went on talking to whoever it was she was talking to in a slightly lower voice so that, while he could hear her, he couldn't understand what she was saying.

He got out of bed, listening intently, and it was clear that she was not in his room, her room or even in the house. She was outside. He opened the door, hurried down the stairs and out into the garden. When he reached it, he discovered that it was nothing like the actual, daytime garden that surrounded the house, but rather something like the maze at Hampton Court, for it seemed to consist entirely of thick, tall hedges set at odd angles to one another. Since Sara had sounded so annoyed when he called to her, he did not call again but tried to find her by walking toward the sound of her voice. But every time he thought he knew where she was, he would run into a hedge and have to go in a different direction to get around it. Then, when he was close enough to hear what she was actually saying, convinced that she was just on the other side of the hedge ahead of him, he woke up.

He woke, blinking at the morning sun that had awakened him and smiling. For a moment he was puzzled. He remembered the dream very clearly, and there was nothing about it that should make him feel particularly good because he never did actually find Sara. Then he suddenly realized why he felt the way he did. It was because *Sara* had sounded so cheerful, completely relaxed and gay, even laughing once or twice.

Though he was no longer smiling when he stopped in at his mother's room on his way downstairs for breakfast, he was still in good enough spirits so that she said, "You seem fairly cheerful this morning."

"I am."

"Any reason for it?"

"No. It's just that everything's been so bad so far that I've a feeling something good's finally going to happen."

"That would be a nice change."

When he got down to Scotland Yard, Wyatt looked up from the papers on his desk, nodded to him, then looked at him more closely.

"Well, well. Do you know something I don't?" he asked.

"No."

"Then why do you look as if you've been reading Samuel Smiles?"

"I don't know. Yesterday you said there was a rhythm to cases. Well, I think that it's going to change. That something good's going to happen today."

Wyatt continued to look at him. "The Latin word for it is *auspex*, someone who finds or recognizes favorable auguries or signs, from which we get out word auspicious. Something *has* happened."

"What?"

"Some of the shoful money has turned up."

"The counterfeit money mother left in Regent's Park?"

"Yes."

"Where?"

"Where we knew it would eventually—at one of the banks."

"But who had it? Who turned it in?"

"That's what Tucker's gone to find out. We'll know when he gets back. Now be quiet and let me try and do something about some of my other cases."

Andrew sat down in one of the hard wooden chairs and tried to control his impatience while Wyatt continued to read the papers in one of the folders on his desk, making an occasional note on a pad. Luckily it was only a few minutes before they heard the sergeant's heavy tread outside, and he came in.

"I see the full choir's here," he said, glancing at Andrew.

"Yes," said Wyatt. "What's the gen?"

"It was turned in by someone they knew, the landlord of a pub."

"Which pub?"

"The Four Bells, near Belgrave Dock. The landlord's name is Cutter, Jem Cutter. He used to be a pug, a pretty useful light heavyweight."

"I don't suppose you were able to go any further than that."

"You don't, eh? You know what time I left here. Where do you think I've been ever since?"

"Bending your elbow somewhere."

"If I was, it was in the line of duty."

"And?"

"I went over and talked to Cutter. He was as mean as measles at first. The bank had kept the queer ten bob, and he thought he was out it. So I gave him ten out of me own poddy pocket."

"Just like that? You're a trusting soul."

"I am that. I thought the Yard was good for it. Well, that sweetened him up something wonderful, and yes, he remembered where he got the ten. It was from a tosher named Ernie, who's one of his regulars."

"What's a tosher?" asked Andrew.

"A scavenger who works in the sewers," said Wyatt, "picking up odds and ends and sometimes things that are quite valuable. It's illegal because it's dangerous. Toshers can be trapped down there and drowned or asphyxiated. But since they're useful to the police—they often find things we're looking for, like weapons—we close our eyes and let a few old-timers go on with what they've been doing for years. Any idea where we can find this Ernie?" he asked Tucker.

"At The Four Bells. If not now, then later."

Nodding, Wyatt got up. "Where do you think you're going?" he asked Andrew when he got up too.

"You know very well where. With you."

"Do you really think it's proper for me to take someone of your tender years to a pub?"

"Since you've already done it several times—and the sergeant took me to one yesterday for lunch—it's too late to worry about it. Besides, you're going to need me."

"Are we?"

"Yes."

"As a loyal Roman, I never argue with an *auspex*. All right. Come along."

Since they couldn't all ride in a hansom—the sergeant was much too big—Wyatt hailed a four-wheeler on the Embankment and told the cabby where they wanted to go.

The Four Bells proved to be a typical waterman's pub, dark and dingy and not too clean. Two seamen, probably wherrymen, sat in one corner smoking short clay pipes, but outside of that, the pub was empty. Even if the sergeant hadn't told them that the landlord had been a prizefighter, Andrew would have known it from his broken nose and thickened ears. Despite his forbidding appearance, he was quite friendly, waving to the sergeant when they came in; and since it was Tucker who had bought his good will by returning the ten shillings he had thought he had lost, Wyatt sent him over to get pints for the two of them and some ginger beer for Andrew. When he came back, he told them that Ernie had not been there yet, which puzzled the landlord, but when he did arrive the landlord would let them know.

"This really is important, isn't it?" asked Andrew.

"It can be," said Wyatt. "If this Ernie can tell us where he got the counterfeit ten bob, we will have moved that much closer to whoever sent the ransom note and is holding Sara and Maria."

"Are we absolutely certain that whoever it is, is holding Maria too?"

"Because her mother won't admit she's missing? I'll give you twenty to one that she *is* missing, and that's the reason she is."

"I suppose it does make sense," said Andrew. "I mean, if her father's a count, he's probably quite rich, and—"

He broke off as the pub door opened and a strange-looking old man shuffled in. He was stooped and gray-bearded. He wore a dark watch cap, a long corduroy jacket with enormous pockets, canvas trousers and boots —and he smelled; smelled so malodorously that even though they were across the room from him, Andrew winced. Muttering to himself and clearly in a rage, the old man slammed a coin down on the bar and, when the landlord served him, went off to sit by himself in the far corner of the pub. The landlord caught Tucker's eye, and the sergeant went over, talked to him for a moment, and then came back.

"That's not Ernie," he said quietly, "but he's a friend of his. Another tosher named Abner; Cutter says he'll be able to tell you about Ernie."

Wyatt nodded and went over to the old man.

"Your name's Abner?"

"What if it is?"

"I understand that you're a friend of Ernie's."

"What?" The old man looked him up and down with fierce blue eyes. "Who the devil are you?"

"My name's Wyatt. I'm an inspector attached to Scotland Yard."

"Oh, you are, are you? Well, what do you want with me?"

"I'd like to ask you a few questions about Ernie."

" 'Strewth! You mean you're still going on about that? I was with your blue boys at the Pimlico station all morning, and I told them all I knew!"

"About what?"

"About Ernie! Isn't it enough that he's dead? That—"

"What did you say?"

"I said that Ernie was dead. You mean you didn't know it?"

"No, I didn't. When did he die?"

"I don't know exactly when, sometime last night. They found his body down near the river this morning. Some murdering sod had stuck a shiv between his ribs."

"And the police don't know who?"

"No. They kept asking me about it, but I told them I didn't know anything, never saw him after I left here at six last night."

"I see. I'm sorry about it, very sorry."

The old tosher had drained his glass, and catching the landlord's eye, Wyatt jerked his head. When the landlord brought over another gin, Tucker and Andrew came over too, and all three of them remained there as Wyatt continued talking to Abner.

"He was your friend?"

"Yes," said the tosher in a husky voice. "He was me cully."

"I told you I'm from Scotland Yard. I'm working on a case that Ernie may have had something to do with. If you can help me, tell me some things I need to know, it may be that I'll be able to find out who killed Ernie."

"I'll help. I'll do anything I can to help."

"Do you know who gave him the ten bob note he gave Jem Cutter here?"

"When was this? When did he give it to you?" he asked the landlord.

"Day before yesterday, kind of latish."

"Let's see. Yes, I think I do know! I'll bet it was that ratty-looking fellow he was drinking with early in the afternoon!"

"Can you tell me anything about him?"

"Just that he was small and dark, with a thin face and a funny kind of smile—the kind that isn't a smile at all. When I come in, Ernie's sitting here and drinking with this fellow and he tips me a wink and shakes his head so I go off and sit by myself. Then the fellow goes, and Ernie comes over and he won't tell me what it was all about but he's merry as a mouse in a maltbin, and he says the drinks is on him."

"Yes, that sounds possible," said Wyatt. "You can't tell me any more than that—where Ernie met this man or how?"

"No," said Abner.

"I can tell you his name," said the landlord. "His first name anyway. It was Sam."

"How do you know?" asked Wyatt.

"I didn't remember him until Abner here said he was kind of ratty-looking and had a funny smile. Then I did —and I also remember going over and having Ernie say, 'My friend Sam here is paying for these.' "

"I see. Well, that's a help." Wyatt glanced at Tucker, who nodded.

"You think maybe he's the one who done old Ernie in?" asked the tosher.

"I don't know. We'll do some checking. Will you be here for a while?"

"Yes. I ain't doing no toshing today. Me heart wouldn't be in it."

"I understand. Well, perhaps we'll see you later."

Wyatt settled with the landlord, thanked him, and they went out.

"Well, Sergeant?" said Wyatt.

"The description sounds like the one Dodson gave us of the cove who was watching to see that the first ransom note was delivered."

"Right. And now we know that his name is Sam. Will you check records again?"

"As soon as we get back to the Yard."

They separated when they got there, the sergeant going to the central records room and Andrew and Wyatt up to the inspector's office.

Wyatt had been very quiet while they were in the four-wheeler, and he remained silent for some time after they got to the office, sitting at his desk with his chair tipped well back and staring blankly at a point high up on the wall. Finally, looking sideway at Andrew, he said, "I'm afraid I'm not being very entertaining."

"That's not exactly what you're supposed to be, is it?"

"No. I'm supposed to solve crimes, but I'm not doing particularly well in that department either. At least, not with the case I'm most concerned about."

"Don't you think you're getting anywhere at all with it?"

"I don't know. As Tucker said, it looks as if the chap who watched to make sure the ransom note was delivered to your house was the same man that Ernie had drinks with. And of course it was probably he who gave Ernie the counterfeit ten bob that Ernie gave Cutter. But though we've got more facts now than we had before, they don't quite fit together."

"That's what I was thinking. Not just that they don't fit, but that there are too many of them. It's like trying to fix a broken clock and thinking you've put it together and then discovering you've got parts left over. I can understand why whoever sent Harry the bootblack to pick up the money would want to keep him quiet. But why should this person—and it probably was the same person since he used a knife in both cases—why should this person kill an old tosher, and what does that have to do with Maria's father's trip or King Alexander's visit or—"

Wyatt's chair, which had been tipped back on two legs, came down on all four with a crash.

"Oh, my sainted aunt!" he said, jumping to his feet. "If Tucker gets back before I do, keep him here!" and he was out of the office before Andrew could blink, much less ask him what had struck him so suddenly.

Tucker came in a few minutes later, his notebook in his hand.

"Where's his nibs?" he asked.

"I don't know. He said if you came back before he did, you were to wait here."

"But you've no idea where he went?"

"No. He was sitting there with the grumps about the way things were going when suddenly he jumped up, said I was to keep you here and went running out."

Tucker nodded gravely. "That's it, then. It happens almost every time. He'll be sitting there all dumpish because he's such a dunderhead, and suddenly he'll jump up like a bee stung him and he's got the answer." He paused. "Are you hungry?"

"A little."

"So am I. If he's not back in ten minutes, one of us'll slip out and bring back something for our lunch. Some Scotch eggs, maybe. Or perhaps some cheese and pickles. Do you like cheese and pickles?"

"Yes."

"So do I. Not as much as a beef sandwich, of course, but . . ."

Wyatt returned with what looked like several rolled-up maps or charts.

"So you're back," he said to Tucker. "Find anything?"

"Yes, sir."

"Good. You can tell us about it on the way. Forward, the Greys!" And he swept them out ahead of him.

"Where are we going?" asked Andrew.

"Back to The Four Bells."

He hailed another four-wheeler, and when they were bowling west along the Embankment for the second time that morning, "Well, sergeant?" he asked.

"Does the name Barney Barnett mean anything to you?"

"Of course. He was the best known fence in London for about twenty years. But he's dead."

"Right. Died three years ago. But his widow, Addie Barnett's still alive. There are those that said she was the real brains of the combination, told Barney what to do and how to do it. And there have also been some rumbles that she's taken over Barney's pitch and expects to do even more with it than he did, spread out into other things besides fencing."

"That's interesting. But what's it got to do with our friend Sam?"

"Barney had a demander and enforcer named Sam, sometimes called Smiling Sam. You know what that kind is usually like."

"Ex-pugs or wrestlers, physical types who'll black your eye or break your arm, as easy as kiss my hand."

"Right. Well, Sam isn't like that. He's little and dark, but the word is that the coves were more afraid of him than of the biggest bully that ever was. Because, besides Smiling Sam, he was also called Sam the Shiv, and he's supposed to be as mean as a starving stoat."

"I gather the thought is that he's now working with Addie Barnett."

"That's it."

"What's she like, this Addie Barnett?" asked Andrew.

"Probably in her fifties, wears a red wig, limps a little so that she has to use a cane and smokes cigars."

"They sound like an endearing pair," said Wyatt.

"Do you think they're the ones who have Sara and Marie?" asked Andrew.

"If they don't actually have them, they were certainly involved in the kidnapping."

"For ransom?"

"No. I think there's more than that involved—a lot more."

"Like what?"

"There are some things I want to look into. When I've done that, if you haven't guessed, then I'll tell you."

That was all he seemed to want to say, and knowing him, neither Andrew nor the sergeant pressed for more.

When they entered The Four Bells, they saw that Abner was still there, as he had said he would be. And though the pub was fairly full now, either because most of those there knew him and knew he wanted to be alone or because of the way he looked and smelled, he was sitting by himself in the corner where they had left him, staring morosely at his hot gin and lemon.

"Can I ask you some more questions?" said Wyatt, sitting down opposite him.

"Oh, it's you again," said the old tosher. "Ask away. If I can tell you what you want to know, I will."

"Did you and Ernie cover the same beat, work in the same sewers?"

"No. That wouldn't make sense. Each tosher has his own sewer and works that. I been at it longer than anyone, so I got one of the best, the main one that runs back from Pimlico Pier."

"And Ernie?"

"He worked one that branched off it to the right."

Wyatt nodded as if that was what he had expected and

unrolled what Andrew had thought was a map. It proved
to be a blueprint with a network of white lines on it.

"This is a plan of the London sewer system. Can you
point out Ernie's sewer to me?"

Abner drew back from the blueprint as if he was afraid
it would bite him.

"I don't know nothing about plans," he said.

"A plan is like a map."

"I don't know nothin' about maps neither." Then,
with an effort, "I can't read."

"Oh. Well, you don't have to be able to read to understand a plan or map. For instance," he pointed to the
bottom of the blueprint, "this is the Thames. And these,"
indicating the heavy white lines that ran into it, "these
are the main sewers."

"I still don't know what's what. All I can tell you is
that mine's the one that comes out next to Pimlico Pier."

"That's this one. And Ernie's?"

"I told you. His is the first branch that goes off to the
right."

"That would be this one," said Wyatt, pointing. He
unrolled the second chart he was carrying, and this did
prove to be a map—a large scale map of those parts of
Chelsea and Westminster that lay just north of the
Thames. He compared the map with the blueprint, then
said, "Will you take us into the sewer with you tomorrow and show us Ernie's beat?"

"Who's us?"

"The sergeant and me."

"I'll show it to you, but you won't be able to go into it."

"Why not?"

"Because you're too big. It's all right, almost as big as mine later on, but where it comes into the main sewer there's a squinchy little place that you couldn't get through in a hundred years."

"Could I get through?" asked Andrew.

The tosher studied him.

"You're about Ernie's size. Yes, you could get through."

"I don't remember suggesting that you come along," said Wyatt.

"You didn't, but I told you you'd need me."

Wyatt looked at him, then at Tucker.

"Height requirements," said the sergeant. "We don't have any constables that small. I could probably find a boy who's done some work with us—"

"Haven't I worked with you?" asked Andrew angrily. "Besides, if it has anything to do with Sara, you're *got* to let me come along!"

Again Wyatt looked at him.

"All right. You can start out with us anyway. We'll see whether you go into the branch sewer or not." He turned back to Abner. "When do we meet, and where?"

"Low tide's a little after six tomorrow. We'll meet at

six just back of Pimlico Pier. But there are things you'll need, boots and duds and so on."

"I've got boots," said Andrew. "What else?"

"Bull's-eye lanterns and poles."

"I know about a tosher's pole," said Tucker. "I'll get those. And the lanterns and duds."

"You'd better discuss this particular expedition with your mother," said Wyatt to Andrew. "If it's all right with her, we'll pick you up at five fifteen. And we'll meet you back of the pier at six," he said to Abner.

The old tosher nodded unhappily. "No more Ernie," he said. "Don't seem right. Things ain't going to be the same without him."

12

The Sewer

Wyatt admitted later on that Andrew had handled the matter very well. He took Andrew home and waited while Andrew talked to his mother, telling her that because of a new development in the case, which he didn't completely understand, Wyatt and Tucker were going down into the sewers the next morning with an old tosher. He wanted to go with them but Wyatt had said that he must get her permission first. He had to pause and explain what a tosher was and then went on to say that of course he'd wear old clothes, but even then he'd probably smell awful and need a bath when he got back, as if that were Wyatt's only reason for insisting that he get her permission. Verna looked at Wyatt and said that if Andrew didn't understand the significance of the new development, it wasn't likely that she would, so she wouldn't ask him about it. And since she assumed that

Andrew would not be in any danger—because if there were any, Wyatt would not let him go, permission or no—it would be all right for him to go.

So that's how it was that Andrew was waiting under the porte-cochere at a little after five the next morning when a four-wheeler rumbled up through the misty, before-dawn greyness, and Wyatt opened the door and told him to get in. Andrew had been afraid he would oversleep, even after Annie the parlormaid had assured him that she was always up at a quarter of five and would wake him. When he had first gotten into bed, so many things had been going through his head—anxiety about Sara, speculation about what Wyatt expected to find in the sewers—that he was convinced he would never fall asleep. But as it turned out, one fear was as groundless as the other. He did fall asleep at last and was already up and almost dressed when Annie knocked at his door. He apologized to cook, who had been very upset when he told her he couldn't wait for breakfast, and was greatly relieved to hear that neither Wyatt nor Tucker had had any either. The result was that they stopped at a stall on Marylebone Road, and they and the cab driver all had mugs of tea and buns at which cook would have turned up her nose, but which Andrew thought were very good.

They were at the meeting place back of Pimlico Pier at a little before six, and Abner was already there. He was wearing the same outfit he had worn the day before:

boots, watch cap, long corduroy jacket and canvas trousers. But now he had a bull's-eye lantern strapped to his chest, and he carried a gunnysack and a pole about six feet long with an iron hoe fastened to the end of it.

He watched as the cabby handed down three similar poles from the rack on top of the four-wheeler, one a little shorter than the others, for Andrew. The poles received his grudging approval, but he was sniffy about the oilskin jackets that Tucker had bought at a ship chandler, pointing out that they only had two pockets while his jacket had six. When Wyatt explained that they weren't actually going to be doing any toshing, only needed the jackets for protection, he shrugged and told them to hurry since they were wasting valuable time. He waited impatiently while they put on their jackets and tied the bull's-eye lanterns to their chests. (When Andrew asked why they did that, he looked at him scornfully and asked him how he expected to do *anything* if he didn't have his hands free.) Then he led the way to a round iron manhole cover just down the street and pried it up with the hoe on the end of his pole. Since it was fairly heavy, Tucker tried to help him, but he scowled and said he'd been lifting the covers since he was a boy and didn't need help from anyone.

When he had slid the cover aside, Andrew saw that an iron ladder, bolted to the side of the round opening, led down into the dark depths below. Taking out a box of lucifers, the old tosher lit his lantern; then, holding his pole and gunny sack in one hand, went nimbly down the ladder. Tucker lit Andrew's lantern, then Wyatt's and his own.

"All right, Andrew," said Wyatt. "Go ahead."

Shortening his grip on his pole, Andrew went down the ladder. As he did, he descended, not just into darkness, but into the most fetid stench he had ever smelled—a full-bodied version of the smell that had come from Abner in the pub. It was so powerful that for a moment his stomach heaved and he thought he was going to be sick. By the time he had gotten hold of himself, Wyatt and Tucker had come down also—Tucker having replaced the manhole cover before he descended.

Fascinated by this new and previously unimagined world, Andrew looked around. He was standing on a narrow walkway at the bottom of a round, brick-vaulted tunnel that was about ten feet high. A few inches below the walkway was a wide channel through which a foul-smelling torrent ran, foaming and gurgling as it carried all the city's soil and waste to the Thames.

Outside of the small area lit by their lanterns, the darkness was absolute, with no other sign of light anywhere.

Old Abner, who had seemed particularly twitchy and irritable before, was now quiet and calm, as if he were only happy here in these nether regions that were peculiarly his own.

This was one of the main sewers, he explained. He would take them to the branch they were interested in—the one Ernie used to work—and then he'd have to leave them because he had his own work to do. But first, there were some things he must tell them.

They should carry their poles at all times. When they came to a narrow place, they could use it to balance with. If they came to a place where the footing was uncertain, they should use the hoe at the end to try the ground before they tried to cross it. And if they should slip and fall into the stream, they should try to hook something with the hoe so as to pull themselves out. But besides these uses, the pole and hoe was also a weapon—and a necessary one. The sewers were overrun by large and ferocious rats, and while it was unlikely that they would be troubled when there were three of them, he—Abner—had been attacked by rats several times when he was alone and had to fight them off with the hoe.

Then, glancing around to make sure they were ready, the old tosher set off along the walkway. Andrew followed him with Wyatt behind him and Tucker bringing up the rear.

Abner walked along slowly, eyes roving, and every few feet he would plunge his hoe into the reeking stream. Like the fishermen Andrew had watched tonging for oysters in Cornwall, he seemed able to feel things he could not see and, with a dextrous twist, would bring them out of the dark and turbid water onto the walkway. Sometimes it was a piece of rusty iron that he would put into his gunny sack. Sometimes it was a bit of china or a pot and once it was a small but heavy canvas bag. Abner was quite excited at this, but when he opened it, it proved to contain a collection of various size nails, probably dropped by a carpenter. Shrugging, the tosher stowed that in his sack too and went on again.

Andrew had been prepared for the darkness and, at least partly, for the smell. What he had not been prepared for was the noise—for the sound of the rushing water was not only loud, but it echoed in the confined space so that it was almost impossible to hear anything else.

On they went, walking carefully in single file on the narrow walkway beside London's own River Styx. At one point, instead of fishing in the torrent with his pole, Abner thrust his hand into a fissure between the bricks at the side of the walkway, felt around and brought out a spoon. He wiped it on his coat and showed it to Andrew. It was dark and tarnished, but it looked as if it were silver and quite old and therefore might be rather valuable. Andrew nodded his congratulations, and Abner grinned as he put it into one of his coat pockets.

Andrew was not sure how long they had been walking—perhaps ten minutes, perhaps a little longer—when Abner stopped again. They had passed a few branches that entered the main sewer on the other side of the stream but now, for the first time, there was one on their side.

Abner put his mouth to Andrew's ear.

"This is it," he said above the noise of the rushing water. "That's old Ernie's branch."

Wyatt and Tucker joined them, and when Wyatt raised an inquiring eyebrow, Andrew nodded. They all looked at it, and it was easy to see why Abner had said that neither Wyatt nor Tucker could get through there. The branch was not only smaller than the main sewer they were in, but the overhead arch had broken down and the opening was more than half-choked with fallen bricks and rubble.

"Wouldn't be much trouble to clear that away," shouted Tucker. "Then we could get through easy."

"Don't you dare touch that!" said Abner excitedly. "You pull out any of those bricks, and the whole roof could come down on you!"

Wyatt examined what was left of the overhead arch by the yellow light of his lantern.

"I'm afraid he's right," he said. "The bricks here do look pretty rotten."

"I still don't know why you want to go in there," said Tucker, "but if it's important, can't we get in from the other side?"

"I suppose so," said Wyatt. "I think this is the branch that runs past Victoria Station, and I imagine that someone in the Board of Works could tell me where the man-holes at that end are."

"There's no need for that," said Andrew. "You may not be able to get through there, but I can."

"Well, you're not going to try," said Wyatt firmly.

"Why not?"

"Because it's too dangerous. If the roof came down with you on the other side, then we'd really be in a pickle." He turned to Abner. "Did Ernie ever tell you how far this branch goes?" he asked.

"No. I know it goes on a good way, then starts to get smaller, but . . ."

As Wyatt talked to the old tosher, Andrew bent down and, with only the slightest effort, wriggled through the partially blocked opening of the branch, dragging his pole behind him.

"Hey, there! Hold on!" said Tucker when he noticed.

"What the devil do you think you're doing?" said Wyatt angrily.

"It's done—I'm through—so stop fussing and tell me what you want me to do," said Andrew.

"I want you to come right back out here again!"

"Well, I won't!" said Andrew. "There's something you wanted done over here or something you wanted to find out—something that has to do with Sara's kidnapping. Now are you going to tell me what it is, what you want, or do I just have to go off on my own?"

Wyatt bent down and looked at him through the small

opening. The lantern cast shadows that made it difficult to read his expression, but it seemed to Andrew that his face was tense.

"All right," he said. "Turn around and tell me what you see."

"The sewer is smaller than the main one," reported Andrew. "I'd say it's about six feet high. There's no walkway here, just a channel on the bottom that's about a foot wide. The roof looks solid enough."

"How far can you see?"

"About a hundred yards. Then the sewer curves to the left and I can't see beyond that."

Wyatt looked down, thinking, then looked up again. "You say the roof looks solid?"

"Yes."

"Any sign of rats?"

"No."

"Then, if you feel up to it, walk to the curve, see what you see on the far side of it, then come back and tell me what you saw."

Holding his pole across his chest as he had seen Abner hold his when he wasn't toshing, Andrew started up the sewer. The water in the channel here was only a few inches deep and made only a faint trickling sound as opposed to the loud and steady rushing of the torrent in the main sewer. As a result, for the first time he could hear, not only the sound of his footsteps echoing in that confined space, but the distant rumble of traffic overhead.

Somehow that made him aware of where he was—down under the city—and with that awareness came fear. For he was not only far down under the street, he was completely alone. Wyatt and Tucker might know where he was, but if he needed them, they couldn't possibly get to him.

One of his feet slipped, and he stepped into the filthy water of the channel, regained his balance and jumped out.

This was silly! Why should he need anyone? He had told Wyatt that the roof looked solid, and it did. It seemed damper than the main sewer—water dripped from the overhead arch and it was blotched with dark discolorations and the horrid green of some kind of moss or mold—but there were no bricks missing as there were at the narrow place where he had crawled through. As for rats . . . Was that something moving ahead of him? No. It was just a shadow. The truth was that there *was* no reason for him to be afraid except that he was alone in a strange and unfamiliar place. And even if there were a good reason for it, he would still go on if there was even a possibility that it might bring Sara back.

He reached the curve in the sewer, paused. About fifty yards past the bend, in the center of the sewer, was a large, dark mass. He looked at it, looked back toward the opening he had come through—the faint glow from the lanterns on the far side made it seem farther away than ever—then slowly went forward again.

Whatever the dark thing was, it wasn't alive because it hadn't moved. And he didn't think it could be anything dead—the body of a man or a large animal—because it was so square. When he got closer, he saw that it was a bundle—about two feet by three feet by a foot high—wrapped in oilskins and raised on pieces of wood so that it was well above the runnel in the center of the sewer. But that was not all. Two heavily coated wires came out of the top of the bundle and ran back down the sewer about twenty or thirty feet, then disappeared through a crack in the sewer's left-hand wall.

Andrew looked down at the bundle. The oilskin was torn in one place. Gripping the edges, he made the tear larger. The oilskin was wrapped around a wooden case. There was some lettering on top of the case. Adjusting his lantern, he bent down and read it, straightened up and hurried back along the sewer to where Wyatt and Tucker were waiting.

"Well?" said Wyatt.

"There's something there—a big, square bundle wrapped in oilskin—about fifty yards past the bend in the sewer."

"Did you look at it closely? Can you tell me anything about it?"

"Yes. I tore the oilskin so that I could see what was inside. There was a crate there, and the lettering on the lid said *Nobel Explosives Company*, N.G. seventy-five. But that's not all. Two wires came out of the top of the

crate and went through a crack in the left-hand wall."
He heard Wyatt draw in his breath sharply. "It's dynamite, isn't it?"

"Yes."

"What's N.G. seventy-five?"

"The strength—seventy-five percent nitroglycerine."

"Is that what you expected to find there?"

"I thought it was likely."

"What are you going to do about it?"

"Deactivate it."

"How?"

"Get in there from the other end of the sewer and
either cut or disconnect the wires."

"Can't I do it?"

"No!"

"Why not?"

"Because I don't want you to! I don't want you to
go near it again!"

He could hear Tucker, on the other side of Wyatt,
saying something about time.

"If time is important, then you've *got* to let me do it,"
said Andrew. "If you don't, you've got to go to the
Board of Works, find out where the manhole at the other
end is, and come back down the sewer from who knows
where. Besides, isn't dynamite supposed to be fairly safe
to handle?"

"Dynamite is, but a detonator isn't." Wyatt paused.
Andrew still couldn't see his face clearly through the

small opening, but he could see that his jaw was clamped shut and he could also see the gleam of sweat on his forehead. Then, abruptly," All right," he said. "Will you do exactly what I tell you to do? But exactly?"

"Yes."

"Do you have a knife?"

"No."

Again Tucker said something, and his hand came through the opening holding out a large pocket knife.

"Careful with it," he said. "It's sharp."

Andrew nodded and took it.

"The first thing I'd like you to do," said Wyatt, "is pace off the distance to the bend in the sewer and then the distance to the place where the wires come out of the wall. Here's a notebook and pencil." He passed them through the opening. "Write the figures down."

"Right."

"About the dynamite, you're not going to handle it, so there shouldn't be any danger. You needn't cut both wires. One will be enough. After you've cut it, twist the cut wire around the other one so that it doesn't look as if it's been disturbed. Got that?"

"Yes. If anyone looks at it, you want them to think it's the way it was."

"That's it. All right. Go ahead." His voice rose a little. "And hurry!"

Andrew nodded. Though Wyatt had said that there was no danger in what he was going to do, he knew that the reason Wyatt had told him to hurry—and the reason his voice had gone up—was that he was worried.

Turning, and trying to keep all his steps the same length, he began pacing off the distance to the bend in the sewer. He had thought it was about a hundred yards. It turned out to be ninety-two paces. He wrote the figure down in the notebook, then paced off the distance to where the wires came out of the sewer wall. Fifty six paces.

He put the notebook and pencil in his pocket, took out Tucker's knife and opened it. Wyatt had said that though dynamite was safe to handle, a detonator wasn't. He knew that a lit fuse or an electric spark could set it off. What else could—hitting or shaking it? He didn't know, but he decided to be very careful.

He separated the two wires, noting that though his mouth was dry, his hand was steady. Then, holding one wire against the wooden crate, he cut through it quickly and cleanly.

He had not realized he had been holding his breath until his chest began to hurt and he let it out with a sigh. Twisting the cut wire around the other one, he pushed both of them inside the covering oilskin, then hurried back down the sewer at a pace that was almost a run.

"All right," he said when he reached the small opening that led into the main sewer.

"Done?"

"Yes." Pushing his pole ahead of him, he bent down

and started to crawl through the hole, but as soon as his head appeared, Wyatt took him by the shoulders and pulled him through—as if he couldn't get him back to where he belonged soon enough.

"Good show!" he said, his voice a little husky.

"Yes, good as ever went endwise!" said Tucker, slapping him on the back. "Were you nervy?"

"Yes, a little. I'm still not sure I understand what it's all about."

"You will," said Wyatt. He looked around. "Where's Abner?"

Tucker pointed to the old tosher, who had lost all interest in what they were doing and was continuing his scavenging up the sewer. Wyatt waved to him and, somewhat reluctantly he came back toward them.

"We're going," said Wyatt.

"Going where?"

"Back. Out of the sewer."

Abner stared at him, puzzled. "But it's still early. You just got here, and . . ." He suddenly remembered who they were, why they were there. "Did you find what you wanted?"

"Yes."

"Is it gonna help you find out who done Ernie in?"

"It may."

"I want to see him scragged, whoever done it! Think you can find your way back to the manhole?"

"I think so. Thanks, Abner."

He waved a disclaimer, turned and went back up the sewer, fishing in the drain as he went. They went the other way, walking quickly in single-file. They had no difficulty in finding the manhole. Tucker went up the ladder first and lifted the heavy metal cover. Andrew followed him, and Wyatt came last.

Andrew looked around as Tucker replaced the manhole cover. They had been down in the sewer for less than an hour, but it seemed much longer than that. And though London has never been known for its salubrious air, after the reek of the sewer, the deep breaths they took seemed as fresh as a seaside breeze; and after the noise down there, the city seemed oddly quiet.

"I don't think we'll need these anymore," said Wyatt, untying his lantern and blowing it out, "but perhaps we'd better keep them just in case."

"Give it to me," said Tucker, "and your pole. I'll leave them at The Four Bells." He took Andrew's pole and lantern also. "Where will you be?"

"Over that way," said Wyatt, pointing. "I suspect on Claverton Street."

Tucker nodded and went off toward the pub. Wyatt took out the sewer plan, studied it for a moment, then said, "Have you got my notebook and the distances you paced off?"

Andrew gave it to him and Wyatt opened the notebook.

"The first distance from the beginning of the branch to the curve in the sewer was ninety-two paces?"

"Yes."

Wyatt walked north to the first cross street.

"All right. Count off ninety-two paces for me."

Andrew began walking east on the cross street, trying to keep his paces even and counting as he went. When he reached ninety-two, he stopped.

"Here," he said. He looked around. He was almost exactly in the center of Claverton Street, about a half-block north of the Serbian Embassy. "You knew that this was where it would take us, didn't you?"

"Yes," said Wyatt. "But I wanted to check your paces, make sure that they're the same length now as they were down there. Now comes the important measurement." He looked at the notebook. "The distance to where the wires went through the left-hand wall of the sewer was fifty-six paces?"

"Yes."

"Come over here." Wyatt led him to the curb, then lowered his voice. "Start pacing and counting from here, but don't look down. Try to look as if we're just walking up the street and talking."

Andrew nodded and began walking north on Claverton Street. Since it was a respectable, residential street, it was quiet at that hour of the morning. A brougham waited a short distance ahead of them. As they approached it, a top-hatted gentleman came out of the house, got into it, and the coachman drove off. A green-grocer's delivery boy, carrying a basket of vegetables, came down the other side of the street whistling. Andrew had been counting to himself. When he got to number 56, he paused for a moment and said, "Here."

Wyatt glanced to his left across the street and Andrew followed his glance. The house that they were opposite, number 169, was Georgian—as were most of the houses on the street—but it wasn't quite as well-kept as its neighbors. The pavement in front of it was swept, the brass doorknob and knocker were polished, and there were curtains in the windows of the parlor floor; but the bricks of the facade were discolored and could do with a scrubbing, the trim around the windows needed painting, and there were no curtains on the windows of the upper floors.

"Keep walking," said Wyatt.

"That's the house where the wire went, isn't it?" asked Andrew.

"If your measurements were correct, and I'm fairly sure they were."

"So am I."

"All right. We'll turn around now and go back, but don't look at the house as we go by. Look at me, and pretend I'm telling you something fascinating."

"I wouldn't have to pretend if you told me what this

is all about. It was easy to guess that that's where the wire to the dynamite went, but I'm not sure I understand anything else."

"You will," said Wyatt. They were almost at the cross-street now, and Tucker came hurrying around the corner, stopped when he saw them.

"It's number one sixty-nine," said Wyatt quietly. "I want a watch kept on it, two plainclothes men—the best we've got—in front and two more in the back if there's a rear exit. Clear?"

"Yes, Inspector."

"If you're going to the Yard to get them, take a cab. We've no time to waste."

Tucker nodded and hurried off toward the Embankment.

"As for us," said Wyatt to Andrew, "we're going back to The Four Bells to get cleaned up a bit. Then we're going to pay a call."

13

The Young King

"What day is today?" asked Maria.

Sara, painstakingly writing another note, did not look up.

"Wednesday."

"I don't think so. I think it's Thursday."

Finishing the note, Sara did look up. Maria was reading *Raphael's Almanac*, the battered and torn *Prophetic Messenger and Weather Guide* that she had found in one of the bureau drawers.

"I think it's Wednesday, but what difference does it make?"

"All the difference in the world," said Maria. "If today's Wednesday, then according to Raphael's Everyday Guide, we should avoid letters and writing and keep quiet. But if it's Thursday, then today is a most auspicious day and we will accomplish all that we've set our hearts on."

"I still say it doesn't make any difference."

"Why not?"

"Because I don't believe any of that stuff, and even if I did, it wouldn't matter because the book's three years old."

"You don't believe it?"

"No."

"I'm surprised at you. There are three or four pages of Raphael's predictions here that came true."

"Like what?"

"Well, in the issue before this one he said that February was a dangerous time for travelling, and on February fourteenth there was a train wreck in New Jersey in the United States and seven people were killed and many injured."

"Oh, me! Oh, my!" said Sara ironically.

"You don't think that proves it?"

"No. But even if I did think so, I ask you again what good it'll do when the book's three years old?"

"Why should that make a difference?"

"Because the stars are different each year, so that whatever they stand for will be different."

"Oh. Well, maybe. I was just looking for something to make us feel better."

"Well, maybe this will." And she gave Maria the note she had written with her crude pen and homemade ink on another blank page from the Bible.

"To whom it may concern," it said. "Take this note to Count Michael Milanovitch at the Serbian Embassy, Claverton Street, and he will give you a handsome reward. Maria Milanovitch and Sara Wiggins."

"How much would you say was a handsome reward?" asked Maria. "Five pounds? Ten?"

"I'll leave that to your father. Outside of that do you think it's all right?"

"Oh, yes. Fine," said Maria, giving it back to her.

"All right, then," said Sara. And wrapping the paper around a knob she had unscrewed from the chest of drawers, she tied it with another strip of cloth torn from her petticoat. Then, opening the west window this time and gauging the distance carefully, she threw it and had the satisfaction of seeing it clear the edge of the roof and drop down toward the wide street at the end of the alley.

There were two constables stationed outside the door of the Serbian embassy when Andrew and Wyatt went there this time. One of them must have known Wyatt, for he saluted immediately, and after a whispered word, the other followed suit. Andrew glanced at Wyatt as he rang the bell. Though they had cleaned up and left their oilskin jackets at the pub, they still looked rather raffish, for they were both wearing old clothes and wellingtons. However, since Wyatt didn't seem the least bit disturbed about it, Andrew didn't see why he should be.

The door was opened by the same liveried porter they had seen on their last visit. Again Wyatt presented his card and asked to see Count Milanovitch. Possibly because of their appearance, the porter was even more reluctant to admit them than he had been the last time. But when Wyatt made it clear by his manner that he would not tolerate any delay or equivocation, the man took the card and disappeared through an ornate door to the left of the entrance hall.

He came out a moment later, held the door open and said, "The count will see you in here, Inspector."

Wyatt walked past him, followed by Andrew. They found themselves in a somber office that had once been either a library or a study. Standing in front of the large desk was a tall man who wore a tweed travelling suit rather than the accepted diplomatic dress of tailcoat and striped trousers. He was probably in his late thirties but, possibly because his face was drawn and tired, he looked older than that.

"Good morning, Inspector," he said with no trace of an accent.

"Good morning, Count. It was good of you to see us so promptly."

The count shrugged. "I always assume that Scotland Yard's business is urgent. Though"—he glanced at Andrew—"I did not realize that you had anyone on the force who was quite so young."

"He's not, of course, with us officially," said Wyatt, acknowledging the jest with a smile, "but young as he is, he has been very helpful to us on several occasions. I think you will understand his presence when I tell you why I am here. Meanwhile, may I introduce Andrew Tillett? Count Milanovitch."

"I'm happy to meet you," said the count, bowing politely. "I assume that you're here to review the arrangements for King Alexander's protection."

"Not exactly. I take it that His Majesty has arrived?"

"Yes. At about nine this morning. You say that that is not what you wanted to see me about?"

"No. I've met with Sir Roger and the Special Branch, and I am of course familiar with all the security arrangements. But what I wanted to talk to you about was your daughter, Maria."

The count stiffened. "What do you know about Maria?" he asked in a strained voice.

"I know that, in spite of what your wife says, she has been kidnapped."

"That . . . that's ridiculous!"

"Will you stop that, Count?" said Wyatt angrily. "I saw your wife immediately after it happened, and I was willing to make allowances for her state of shock and the fact that she was terrified. But you . . . Don't you know by now who you can trust?"

"I . . . I'm not sure."

"Well, you should be. And if Sir Roger and the

Foreign Office trust me, you should be able to also. Now I say again, she's been kidnapped, hasn't she?"

His face even paler than it had been, the count studied him for a moment then making up his mind, he said, "Yes. How did you know?"

"Because another girl, a friend of Andrew's here, has been kidnapped too. That's how he became involved in the case, why he's here with me."

"I see."

"When I last saw your wife, she said that you had gone up to Scotland. Was that true?"

"Yes."

"Did your trip have anything to do with Maria's kidnapping?"

"In a sense, yes."

"Tell me."

"The first note we got said that she had been kidnapped, warned us not to go to the police and said that instructions would follow. The second note came almost immediately after and told me to take a thousand pounds to Edinburgh. Further instructions would be waiting for me in a note left for me at the Royal Caledonian Hotel."

"What were the instructions?"

"To put the money in a bag and leave it in the cloak room of the Waverly Station. Then to bring the claim ticket back to the hotel and leave it there in an envelope for Mr. Barney."

"Which you did."

"Yes."

"I'll wire the Edinburgh police and have them pick up the money."

"Have them . . . ? Don't you think the kidnappers have it by now?"

"It's possible, but I doubt it. The purpose of the exercise was not to get the money, but to get you out of London."

"I don't understand."

"You will. You were gone for how long, two days?"

"A little more than that. I just got back about an hour ago." He glanced down at his clothes. "As you can see, I haven't had a chance to change."

"Yes. In the meantime, the arrangements for His Majesty's visit to the queen remain the same?"

"Yes. He's due at Buckingham Palace at five o'clock."

"Will anyone else be riding in the carriage with him?"

"Yes, of course. I will be."

"It's possible that you will not."

"I beg your pardon? Why not?"

"I'll explain that when I explain everything else to you."

"Which will be when?"

"Probably this afternoon. But first, there's something I want you to do for me."

"If it will help to bring back my daughter, I will do anything!"

"That's what the kidnappers counted on."

"Do you know who they are? Where she is?"

"I think so."

"And . . . and you also think . . .?"

"I'm quite sure that we can get her back for you safe and sound."

"Then . . . what do you want me to do?"

"I talked to your assistant, the second secretary, while you were away. His name is Gradowsky, isn't it?"

"Yes, Count Gradowsky."

"I'd like to talk to him again. Would you have him come in here?"

"Of course." He tugged three times at the bellpull on the wall. "That is his ring. It will bring him in without my having to send for him."

"Very efficient. Now, sir," he looked intently at the count, making certain that he had his full attention, "this is important. Do you have work to do, paper work?"

"As you can see." The count nodded toward his desk. "A great deal of work."

"Good. Then sit down there and become busy—as if we've concluded our discussion. And this is the important part. *No matter what I say to Gradowsky, do not act surprised.* Clear?"

The count returned Wyatt's glance, looking at him just as intently as Wyatt had looked at him. His eyes widened slightly, as if he were beginning to understand something that had puzzled him. He nodded, sat down at his desk and busied himself with the papers on it.

"The same thing applies to you, of course," said Wyatt turning to Andrew. "No surprise. But there's something else. You know how I like Tucker to keep his eye on anyone I'm talking to so that we can compare notes later?"

Andrew did know. He'd been present several times when Wyatt was questioning someone and had been interested in the way the two men worked together. For while Tucker sat unobtrusively off to one side with his notebook open on his knee, he was not merely taking notes. He was also watching the person who was being questioned, and being outside the subject's field of vision, he sometimes saw something—a reaction or small involuntary movement—that Wyatt might have missed.

Before Andrew could answer, there was a perfunctory knock, the door opened, and Count Gradowsky came in. He was dressed exactly as he had been except that today the flower in his buttonhole was a cornflower.

"You wanted me, sir?" he asked Milanovitch.

"Hmmm?" The count looked up with pretended abstraction from the paper he was reading. "I didn't, Gregor, but the inspector here did. I gather you know one another."

"Indeed, yes. How do you do, Inspector?"

"Nice to see you again, Count. As you've probably gathered, I came over here to review the security arrangements for His Majesty's visit to the queen this afternoon. When I got here, the count told me that he'd just gotten an urgent message asking him to come over to the Foreign Office for a meeting this afternoon. He'll probably be back in time to accompany His Majesty to Buckingham Palace, but if he isn't, you'll be able to ride over with the king, won't you?"

When Gradowsky came in, Andrew had gone over to the window as if he had no interest in—and of course no connection with—what was happening in the room. But his move was completely unnecessary, for there was nothing subtle about Gradowsky's reaction, nothing anyone could miss. He went white and swayed slightly, his hands gripping one another behind his back as if seeking comfort.

"Go with the king?" he asked in an unsteady voice.

"Yes."

"Of course, if it's necessary, I would be honored to do so. But I wonder if it's advisable." He cleared his throat. "As you can no doubt hear, I seem to have contracted a catarrh or quinsy of the throat, which I suspect may be infectious. And if it is . . ."

"Naturally, the king should not be exposed to it," said Wyatt. "Well, it's not important. If the count hasn't returned in time, there's no reason why His Majesty cannot go alone."

"None," said Gradowsky. "That would certainly be best." He started toward the door, then caught himself, "Was there anything else, Count?"

"No," said Milanovitch. He looked thoughtfully after the second secretary as he left, and though he was frowning, there was a gleam of something else in his eyes when he turned back to Wyatt. "You have found out something you wished to know?"

"Yes."

"But you still do not want to tell me about it."

"Not yet. I would still like to wait until this afternoon."

"Very well." He pushed back his chair and stood up. "I will see you out. It is curious, very curious, how some little thing—even a question—can set one to thinking, make one see something one was not aware of before."

He had opened the door and gestured to Wyatt and Andrew, inviting them to precede him out of the office, when there was a clatter of heels and a young man came running down the flight of marble steps that led to the upper stories of the embassy. He was about sixteen years old, slim and dark-haired. He was wearing boots, breeches and a military tunic, but the collar of his tunic was open, his hair was disheveled, and his dark eyes were bright with excitement.

"Michael, Michael!" he shouted. He began to say something in a Slavic-sounding language, then caught sight of Wyatt and Andrew. "Oh," he said, slowing his headlong descent to a more dignified walk. "I'm sorry. I did not realize you were busy."

"It doesn't matter," said Milanovitch. "May I present Inspector Wyatt of Scotland Yard and Master Andrew Tillett? His Majesty, King Alexander."

"Your Majesty," said Wyatt, bowing.

"I am very happy to meet you, Inspector," said the young king, shaking his hand. "I am a great admirer of Scotland Yard. In fact, I had intended to ask Count Milanovitch if it would be possible for me to visit there."

"It certainly would," said Wyatt. "If you would tell the count when you would like to come, I will make all the arrangements."

"That would be splendid!" said the king. "As for Master Andrew . . ." He hesitated. "Is it Master Andrew or Master Tillett?"

"It depends on who is speaking," said Wyatt.

"No, no. Please do not give me another rule to remember!" said the king with pretended dismay. "If you knew what I have been going through preparing for my visit to your queen. You tell me," he said to Andrew. "What do your friends call you?"

A little dazed by what was happening, Andrew actually had to think before he could answer.

"Just Tillett," he said. "Except for one or two close ones who call me Andrew."

"May I too call you Tillett, then?"

"Why . . . why, yes."

"Thank you. Are you in a great hurry?"

Andrew glanced at Wyatt. "No, Your Majesty," he said.

"Then could we talk for a few minutes? You see, you are the first English person of an age at all close to mine that I have ever met."

"That's astonishing. I mean . . . well, I was wondering where you learned to speak English so well."

"You find I do not speak too badly?"

"I think you speak wonderfully. I wish I spoke anything I'm studying, like French, a quarter as well."

"You're very kind, but I can take little credit for it. You see, I had an English nanny, Miss Dudley, from the time I was very small. And from the age of nine, I had an English tutor, Robert Langham. As a matter of fact, though I did not speak it all the time, I think I spoke English before I spoke Serbian."

"I see."

"Now a question. Do you play cricket?"

"Yes, a bit."

"He's being modest," said Wyatt. "I happen to know that he's very good, a first-rate bowler."

"And I just found out the other day that the inspector is a top flight cricketer," said Andrew. "He won his blue playing for Trinity."

"See?" said the king delightedly to Milanovitch. "You stand there frowning and tapping your foot because you think I am wasting time, mine and the inspector's, but

I have just learned several interesting things. One of them is that we have two cricketers here who will take me to Lord's one of these days to see a match. They are still playing there, are they not?" he asked Wyatt.

"They certainly are. They'll be playing the Test match with Australia there in two weeks."

"I could have told you that," said Milanovitch, who actually did not look at all impatient. "What else have you learned?"

"That if you want to find out anything about a man, do not talk to him—talk to his friend. For would either the inspector or Tillett have told me as much about themselves as each told me about the other?"

"Probably not," said Wyatt. "And now I will let you in on a police secret. The opposite is also true. You can often learn more about a man from his enemy than you can from either a friend or the man himself."

"Yes," said the king, nodding. "I can see that."

"And now, though I am not the least bit impatient, you must not keep the inspector here any longer," said the count.

"Of course. I'm sure he has things to do and I know that you and I have things to discuss," said the king. He turned back to Wyatt. "I cannot tell you how happy I am to have met you," he said, shaking hands with him. "I will see you again?"

"You certainly will—at the Yard and at Lord's.

"And you, Tillett, I'll see you again too?"

"I hope so, Your Majesty."

"The answer is yes, Your Majesty," said Wyatt. "I'll make sure that he's along both times."

"Good," said the king. "Goodbye."

The porter, who had been waiting unobtrusively in the background, opened the door for them. The last glimpse they had of the king as they went out was of him standing next to the count and smiling after them.

14

Questions and Answers

This time, as they left the embassy, both the constables on duty saluted Wyatt simultaneously, and he nodded to them. "We're going back to the Yard," he said to Andrew. "If we walk, it will give us a chance to talk. That is," he glanced sideways at him, "if you haven't forgotten how to talk."

"I beg your pardon?"

"You look, as our friend Sergeant Tucker would say, struck all of a heap."

"Well, I never expected to meet a king. And if I did, I certainly never expected him to be anything like that."

"I know. Nice chap. And as Chadwick said, a good and very important friend of England. And now is everything clear to you? Do you know just what's been going on?"

"I think so."

"Then tell me."

"Well, first of all, it seems to be a plot to kill the king."

"How?"

"By blowing him up with the dynamite we found in the sewer. I'm not sure who's behind it, but apparently someone is waiting in number one sixty-nine, where that wire went, and when the king goes by in his carriage, they intended to set off the dynamite."

"Right. His route, which we've been keeping as secret as we have the time of his visit to see the queen, was to be up Claverton Street, Denbigh Street and Wilton Road to Buckingham Palace. Now go back and fill in some of the details. What did Ernie, the tosher who was killed, have to do with it?"

"If they wanted to place the dynamite in the sewer, they had to have someone who knew the sewers show them how to get where they wanted to go. That would be Ernie. And I suspect that the man he took there, the man who placed the dynamite, was the chap they call Smiling Sam."

"Why do you say that?"

"Well, Abner saw him talking to Ernie, and he and the landlord both said he was a small man, which means he would have been able to get through the narrow place into the branch of the sewer. But besides that, wasn't he known as Sammy the Shiv? So after Ernie had taken him into the sewer—and of course he wouldn't have told Ernie what he wanted to do there—he knifed him to keep him from going to the police—as Ernie certainly would have done after the explosion."

"Right. And of course there are other things linking Sam to the whole plot. Dodson saw him watching your house when Harry the bootblack delivered the first ransom note. And having used Harry once, he used him again to pick up the counterfeit money that was left in Regent's Park. After he had collected it from Harry, he must have stabbed him, intending to keep him from talking, just as he did Ernie."

"But who's behind the whole plot? And what does it have to do with Sara?"

"Well, if Smiling Sam's involved, we know at least one other person who is."

"Addie Barnett, the fence's widow."

"Yes. As to what it all has to do with Sara, we've been over that before, and we agreed that she was kidnapped by mistake. Whether Addie Barnett and Sam made the the mistake or whether they came in later, after someone else did, is unimportant."

"But even if that's true—even if it was really Maria they wanted—I still don't see . . . Wait a minute. I think I do now!"

"Of course you do. Tell me about Maria's father,

Count Milanovitch. Do you think he's loyal to the king?"

"I'm sure he is. Not just loyal to him, but tremendously fond of him. And of course that's the answer. The count helped make all the arrangements for the king's visit to Buckingham Palace, and he would never reveal the details to anyone of whom he was the least bit suspicious. So, if someone wanted to know the plans in advance—what the route was and when he'd be going—the first thing they'd have to do would be to get the count out of the way."

"How?"

"Well, it would have to be something pretty important to get him to leave London at a time like that—his king's first visit to England—but he'd do it to save his daughter. And so, after kidnapping Maria, they sent the count a note saying that in order to protect themselves, they wanted the ransom paid in Edinburgh."

"Right. Which brings us to the question you asked before. Ultimately I'm sure we'll discover that General Petroff, the former regent, is behind the plot. But who else has to be involved in it besides Addie Barnett and Sam?"

"Gradowsky, the second secretary. He was in charge when Count Milanovitch was away—that's why they got Milanovitch away—so that Gradowsky would be in on the plans and pass on the details. And besides . . . That's why you said something about his riding in the carriage with the king, isn't it? Because you wanted to see how he'd react. And he was terrified. Which means that he must know about the bomb!"

"How readily you see through my little strategems, my dear Andrew."

"Not always right away. But . . . all right. I'm clear on everything except for two important things. What are you going to do now? And how are you going to get Sara and Maria back safely? Do you think, for instance, that they're being kept prisoner at one sixty-nine Claverton Street?"

"It's possible, but I doubt it. That's where the wire leads, so there'll be someone there watching to see the king go by and then, when he's some distance up the street and over the dynamite, will expect to set it off. In the confusion that he expects will follow, he—and I think it would probably be Smiling Sam—probably plans to slip out the back way and scarper. But no matter how much damage the explosion did—and it makes my blood run cold to think of what it would have done—we would have been able to trace what was left of the wire to one sixty-nine. And I don't think they want Sara and Maria to be found for a while yet. So, to answer your question about my plans, Tucker and I and—yes, I think it might be interesting to include Milanovitch in the party—will pay a little visit to number one sixty-nine about the time the king leaves for *his* visit to Buckingham Palace. We'll see what we shall see, and one way or another, I'm quite sure that what we find there will lead us to Sara and Maria."

Turning the mirror slightly and tipping it forward on its pivot, Sara looked at herself. Her face was pale, which was not surprising when you considered how many days it had been since she had been out of doors, and she also looked a bit thin. On the whole, however, she didn't think she looked too bad except for her hair. She had always been proud of her hair, which was long and thick and beginning to darken to a becoming chestnut. During the last few months she had been varying the way she wore it, sometimes in a single plait, sometimes in two plaits and sometimes letting it hang loose. But, however she wore it, she had always brushed it at least a hundred times morning and evening. Since her confinement in the attic, however, she had not been able to brush it at all, because she had no brush. In fact, it had taken several days of pleading and of shouting rages to get Zerko to bring her a comb, and her hair was beginning to show it, for it was starting to look limp and lifeless. Shaking it loose, she began combing it for the second time that day, wincing at the tangles.

Maria, stretched out on her cot and reading *Raphael's Alamanac,* glanced up at her.

"What are you doing?" she asked.

"What does it look like?"

"Combing your hair."

"You got it in one."

"It won't do any good. You need a brush to make it look like anything. A hundred strokes, morning and evening."

"I know. That's what I used to do."

"Well, I never exactly did it myself. Or only very rarely. Rose, mother's maid, used to brush it for me in the morning. And, when she was home, mother used to brush it for me in the evening before I went to bed. She said *her* mother had always brushed her hair at night when she was a girl, and . . ."

She broke off as she heard footsteps coming up the stairs. They were too light to be Zerko's, and as they drew nearer and Sara also heard the tap of a cane, she knew who it was. The footsteps stopped, the door was unlocked and opened, and the heavily powdered woman with the red wig, the woman Sara had heard called Addie, came stumping in with her silver-headed cane, followed by the ratlike Sam.

"Well, well," said Addie with a toothy smile. "And how are our two little ducks today?"

"How do you think we are?" asked Sara.

"You should be fine. No lessons, no school, no house-work, nothing to do all day but loll around. When I was your age, I would have thought it was pure heaven."

"I don't doubt it," said Sara. "Because most of the time you were probably out in the streets doing lucifer drops or mumping or buzzing gents' back pockets."

"You're right, my dearie doll, that's just what I used to do," said Addie, her eyes gleaming. "That and worse, much worse. But how do you know so much about it?"

"I told you how."

"So you did. You were born in Dingell's Court, off the Edgeware Road. But what's wrong? Why aren't you happy?"

"Don't try and come it over us like that! You blinking well know why! Locked up here day after day with nothing to do, knowing our folks is worried sick about us—"

"Not true. Not at all true. We've been in touch with them, both your folks, and told them there was no need to worry, that you'd be back with them any day now. As for not having anything to do, maybe you should go over to Mudie's Library, Sam, and get some books for the young ladies. Books about young girls who are locked up in dark towers and rescued by handsome young princes—"

"Oh, would you?" asked Maria eagerly. "Would you get us some books?"

"I might have if you'd behaved different. But if there's one thing I can't stand, it's ungratitude."

"What do you mean?" asked Maria.

"I mean this," said Addie, taking a crumpled piece of paper out of her pocket and holding it up. "Did you ever see it before?"

Sara and Maria looked at it and then at one another.

It was the note Sara had thrown out of the window about an hour before.

"Where'd you get it?" she asked.

"It fell in the street right in front of Zerko when he was out on an errand for me. He had a good idea where it'd come from, so he brought it to me." She took a slim black cigar out of her pocket, put it in her mouth and began rolling up the note. Sam struck a match and held it out to her. She set fire to the note, used it as a spill to light her cigar. Puffing on the cigar, she let the note burn almost to her fingers, then dropped what was left and stepped on it.

"No," she said, smoke jetting from her nostrils, "like I said, if there's one thing I can't stand it's ungratitude. So if you try that, try anything like that again, you'll be sorry—very, very sorry. Do you understand?" she said, thrusting the glowing end of the cigar at Maria's face.

"Yes," said Maria, throwing herself backward, away from it. "Oh, yes. Yes!"

"You leave her alone!" said Sara, advancing on Addie with her fists clenched.

"What?"

"I said, leave her alone! You burn her, and I'll kick you right in the brisket!"

"You know," said Addie, "I think you would. I really think you would. Though what would happen to you if you did," she said, raising her cane and placing the tip against Sara's chest, "is something else again." Shoving hard, she sent Sara staggering backward to thud against the wall, then slide down to the floor. "Remember that!"

She looked balefully at Sara, at Maria, then, puffing on her cigar, she stumped toward the door. Sam opened it for her, then followed her out, slammed and locked it.

Both girls were silent as the footsteps going down the stairs grew fainter, Maria on the cot, Sara still on the floor, rubbing the place where the tip of the cane had jabbed her.

"Well," said Maria, "I guess you were right. Today must be Wednesday."

"What?"

"Don't you remember? If it's Thursday then it's a most auspicious day and we'll accomplish all we've set our hearts on. But if it's Wednesday, then we should avoid letters and writing and keep quiet."

Sara nodded.

15

The Flash

The same two constables were on duty in front of the embassy when Wyatt, Tucker and Andrew got out of the four-wheeler at about twenty to five. Andrew waited until Wyatt had paid the cabby, then said, "How long will you be in there?"

"Just a few minutes, long enough to collect the count."

"And then?"

"We're going to pay our little visit."

"Why can't I come with you?"

"I told you why—not once, but several times! Because we're dealing with some desperate types, and it could be dangerous."

"But . . ."

"Now look, we went over the whole thing before we left the Yard, and you gave me your word that if I let you come this far, you wouldn't keep on pestering me about it. Is that true?"

"Yes."

"Are you going to keep your word?"

"Yes."

"All right, then. Here's the drill. You can wait here and walk up and down, but you're not to come any closer to one sixty-nine than, say, that streetlight." He pointed to a light that was two houses down from number 169. "That'll give you a chance to see the king leave for the palace. Agreed?"

"Yes."

"It might also be better if you didn't say anything to us, didn't follow us as we go up the street to number one sixty-nine."

"All right."

"Good lad."

As Wyatt started into the embassy, Tucker hung back and said under his breath, "It may be hard lines, but he's right. I'll promise you this, though. Once everything's taken care of, I'll come out and get you so you can be with us when we search the place."

"Thanks, sergeant."

The big sergeant slapped him on the back, then joined the inspector, and they went into the embassy together. Andrew watched the door close behind them, then walked slowly up the street. There was a normal amount of activity going on for that time of day. A nursemaid, accompanied by a girl of about five, came up the street pushing an infant in a pram. An underfootman came out of a house across the way and walked toward the corner pillar box with some letters to mail. A victoria came briskly down the street, and a coal dealer's dray lumbered slowly up it, stopping just a few doors past 169. Crossing sweepers were busy at both ends of the street, and Andrew tried to guess which of all the people he could see were what they seemed to be and which, in addition to the uniformed police around the corners, were plainclothes men stationed there by Wyatt and Tucker.

Reaching the streetlight Wyatt had indicated, Andrew paused and looked up the street. Wyatt had said that Sara and Maria were probably not at number 169. But if they weren't, where were they? They could be anywhere in London, and London was very, very big— the biggest city in the world. With a sigh, he turned around and started back toward the embassy.

"What time is that?" asked Maria as the sound of the distant church bell died away.

"Three-thirty," said Sara glibly.

"But that's what you said some time ago."

"Well, I was wrong."

"No, you weren't. But *something's* wrong."

"What do you mean?"

"I think it's four-thirty, not three-thirty, but even if it is three-thirty why haven't they brought us any lunch?"

The Flash

"They forgot. Or else everything's been taken care of with our folks and they've been so busy arranging to let us go they haven't had a chance to bring us lunch."

Maria, still lying on her cot, looked thoughtfully at Sara, and Sara looked away. She had been uneasy ever since the visit of the red-wigged Addie that morning, and as the day wore on, she had become not merely uneasy but convinced that something bad was going to happen. Continuing in her role of protector, she had lied to Maria, trying to make it seem earlier than she knew it was. But she suddenly sensed that Maria not only knew that she was lying, but had become even more worried than she had been because of it. She was on the point of saying something about this when she heard the outside door open and close and footsteps coming up the stairs.

"There you are," she said. "Zerko's coming."

The slow, ponderous footsteps were certainly Zerko's, but there seemed to be another pair accompanying them. They reached the attic, the door was unlocked and opened, and Zerko came in, accompanied by Sam.

"A little late today, aren't you, mates?" said Sara. Then, seeing their empty hands, "Where's our lunch?"

"Lunch?" Sam looked at Zerko, who shrugged. "Well, what do you know? Looks like we forgot it."

"Well, now that you remembered, how about shaking a leg and getting it? And quick! We're fair starved."

"We'll do that, ducky, sure as eggs is eggs, but first we've got to do something else."

177

"Like what?" Then as he took a rag and a length of light rope out of his pocket, "What's that for?"

"What we really came here for was to tell you that everything was fine and dandy and your troubles are just about over."

"You mean you're going to let us go?" said Maria.

"That's it. But we have to make sure you'll behave and keep quiet till we get you where we're supposed to. So"—he advanced toward Sara as Zerko approached Maria—"if you'll hold out your hands so we can tie you up for a while . . ."

Even before Sara saw the look in his eyes, sensed the malevolence that lay behind his smile, she knew he was lying. As he reached for her, she ducked under his hands and ran for the door, but Zerko was in front of it and he lunged for her. Again she ducked, twisted away, but now she was in a corner of the attic and they were both closing in on her. In her extremity she did something she had not done in a long time; she screamed.

When she was younger she had been called Screamer for the best possible reason. Because, not so much if she were frightened or offended as if she was crossed or denied, she would scream in a manner that would make strong men blench. She was older now, her lungs were bigger, and her fear was greater than it had ever been. As a result, her scream was even louder and shriller, so loud and so piercing that Sam and Zerko not only stopped in their tracks, but actually drew back.

"They're lying, Maria!" she shrieked. "Run! Hurry up and get out of here!" And she screamed again, as loudly and devastatingly as before.

Cursing, Sam reached for her and she bit his hand. With a howl, he drew back, and as she opened her mouth to scream again, "Quick, Zerko," he said. "Stop her gob!"

Turning slightly, Zerko struck her a powerful back-handed blow alongside her jaw. Her eyes closed, her knees gave way, and she fell to the floor like a dropped rag doll.

"Bleeding abishag!" growled Sam, nursing his bitten hand. "All right. I'll take care of her. You take care of the other one."

Rigid with terror, Maria watched as he picked Sara up, threw her on the cot and began tying her hands behind her back. Then Zerko had taken some rags and rope from his pocket and was tying her up as Sam was tying up the unconscious Sara. When he had finished, Sam came over and waited as Zerko pushed some rags into Maria's mouth and wrapped a cloth around the lower part of her face so she could not even moan audibly. He tested the lashing on her wrists and, satisfied, led the way to the door. Zerko locked it, and they went down the stairs, past the empty, unfurnished rooms. When they reached the entrance hall, Sam said, "Go on back to the other house. Tell them I'm finishing up here and that I'll be along in a few minutes."

Zerko nodded and left, and Sam lit a lamp and went down into the cellar where he had already assembled the few things he needed for this particular operation: a basin, a plumber's candle, some tow and newspapers, and a large tin of lamp oil. Filling the basin with oil, he floated several handfuls of tow on the surface of the oil, crumpled up the newspapers, spread them around the basin and poured the rest of the oil on them. Then he lit the candle, set it down in the center of the basin and stepped back to admire this simple but effective device he had used before when arson was called for. The candle had been cut so that in fifteen minutes the flame would be close enough to the floating wads of tow to ignite them. (Sam had learned from experience that lamp oil does not ignite as easily as one would think. It requires a wick to burn and that was the function of the tow; to act as a series of wicks.) When the lamp oil itself began burning, it would set fire to the oil-saturated newspapers around the basin, which in turn would set fire to the broken boxes, boards and pieces of wood that he now laid over and around the newspapers. Thus, within a half hour, the cellar would be an inferno, guaranteed to send flames roaring up through the rest of the house, while Sam, who had long since left the premises, was very much in evidence elsewhere.

Sara groaned—or rather tried to groan—and opened her eyes. She had a headache, her jaw, wrists and ankles hurt, and she couldn't seem to move—all of which she found puzzling as well as upsetting until she turned her head and saw Maria lying gagged and bound hand and foot on the cot next to her. Then everything that had happened came flooding back, and while she did not know how long she had been unconscious, she had clear proof that she had been right about Sam and she also knew that she and Maria were in a desperate plight.

Maria's eyes were wide, rimmed with white. She was so terrified that Sara looked away, afraid that her friend's fear would prove contagious and completely immobilize her—Sara; make it impossible for her to do anything to save them both. Not that she wasn't frightened; she was, more frightened than she had ever been in her life. And not that she had the faintest idea of what she could do; but she was determined to do *something*—first because she was furious at red-wigged Addie and that stinking twister, Sam—and second because she had told Maria not to worry, that she—Sara—would take care of her, and finally because it was her nature to be as feisty as a terrier, fight to the bitter end.

Sara looked at Maria again, smiling reassuringly, until she realized that with both of them gagged, Maria couldn't see her mouth anymore than she could see Maria's. Then she rolled over, twisted a little and, putting her feet down on the floor, managed to stand up. With a dancer's agility and balance, she began hopping over to the attic's west window. She was not sure what she intended to do when she got there—break the glass with her head or her elbow and hope someone would hear it?—but it was the closest she could get to any travelled thoroughfare, the only place where she could see anyone. At one point she lost her balance and almost fell, but she was able to catch herself and, even with her bound ankles, managed to reach the window.

She stood there for a moment, breathing hard, and at first she could see nothing at all because the late afternoon sun was shining into her eyes. She moved to one side, leaning against the chest of drawers, and now she could see into the street beyond the roof to the west. Something had evidently just happened there for several people were standing about and looking up the street to the right. She could not see what they were looking at, and as she tried to, pressing her cheek to the glass, she knew that it had all become too much for her and that she was losing her mind, for it seemed to her that she saw Andrew.

She closed her eyes and took a deep breath; and when she opened her eyes again, she could still see him. He was over to her left, just a short distance from the spot where the big building across the alley cut off her view of the street, and he had his back to her. But even if she hadn't recognized his clothes—he was wearing an old jacket and Wellington boots for some reason—she would have known it was Andrew by the shape of his head, the color of his hair, and the way he stood.

"Andrew!" she screamed silently. "Andrew!"

She had heard of people who could read other people's minds, knew what the other person was thinking even when they were miles apart, and it would have been wonderful if Andrew had heard her mute cry, but he didn't, because he didn't move or even turn around.

Sara groaned again, wet with the sweat of effort and tension. To be so close—to actually see him and not be able to reach him in any way—was almost more than she could bear. She *had* to let him know where she was, for Maria's sake as well as her own. She had to!

She leaned hard against the window, as if that would help, and something next to her rattled. She turned and saw her face in the looking glass on the chest of drawers, her eyes narrowed and her brows drawn together with the intensity of her concentration.

The looking glass. The looking glass! Her heart began pounding. Was it possible? She glanced down at Andrew again. He still had his back to her. Hunching over and gripping the top of the looking glass between her chin and her chest, she began to turn it around, being careful not to let it fall off the chest of drawers. She almost had it around—a little more—a little more . . . There. Now it was facing the sun and the street, but the angle was wrong—the reflected rays were hitting high up, near the roofs of the building across the street. Holding the stand in place with her shoulder, she began to push the top of the looking glass forward with her chin. The beam of reflected light moved down, down, until it reached the street just behind Andrew. But he still had his back to her.

"Andrew!" she said silently but intensely. "Turn around!"

Almost as if he had heard her, he *did* turn, and making a last adjustment, she flashed the sun's rays into his eyes.

She saw him blink, raise his hand to shield his eyes and look up to find the source of the disturbing flash.

"It's me, Andrew," whispered Sara. "Me, Screamer!"

His hand still shielding his eyes, he scowled in annoyance and went striding up the street to the right, in the direction that the passersby had all been looking.

Sara felt her strength ebb with her hopes. She did not faint, but her knees gave way and she sank to the floor and remained there, lying on her side, unable to rise, to crawl back to her cot or even to turn over to a more comfortable position.

A short time before this, Wyatt, Tucker and Count Milanovitch had come out of the embassy. Wyatt was not sure how much the count had guessed after their talk that morning, but he did not seem at all surprised to see the inspector when he returned to the embassy. And though he was clearly ready to accompany the king to Buckingham Palace, for he was wearing a formal frock coat and dark striped trousers, he agreed at once to go with Wyatt—and this completely on faith, for Wyatt did not tell him where he was taking him. Wyatt did not know what the count said to the king—he was still up-stairs when they arrived and the count went up to talk to him—but he must have had as much faith in his chargé d'affaires as Milanovitch did in Wyatt, for the count was down again in just a few minutes. Putting on his gleaming top hat, he indicated that he was at the inspector's disposal.

As they went out, the embassy carriage drew up, a dark maroon brougham with the Serbian coat of arms on the door and a footman as well as a coachman in the box. Andrew was waiting in front of the embassy, and he and the count bowed to one another.

"Are we going far?" asked the count as they started north on Claverton Street.

"No," said Wyatt. "Just to that house there." And he nodded toward number 169.

"Oh?" said the count with grim interest, and he said nothing more until they paused in front of the building. Then, looking searchingly at Wyatt, he said, "We are going in?"

"Yes."

"You have not told me who or what we will find there."

"No. Because though I think I know, I am not ab-solutely certain."

"And you have no instructions for me?"

"No. I want you to be completely natural, and I know I can rely on your discretion as well as your intelligence."

"Thank you."

He stepped aside and let Wyatt go up the three steps to the door and rap the brass knocker vigorously against the strike plate. Looking back down the street, Wyatt saw that Andrew was walking toward them slowly and tentatively. After waiting a moment, Wyatt rapped at the door again and a bolt was drawn, the door opened and a large, heavily-bearded man in a coachman's uniform frowned out at them.

"Yes?" he said in a guttural voice. "What you want?"

"Zerko!" said the count before Wyatt could answer. Then, as the bearded man's eyes widened in surprise, Milanovitch said something—or asked him a question—in their native language.

"Who is it, Zerko?" asked another voice as the bearded man hesitated.

Pushing him aside, the count opened the door all the way, revealing a middle-aged, broad-shouldered man with a shaved head who wore a single eyeglass.

"Milanovitch!" he said, staring at the count through his monocle. Then he too said something—or asked a question—in their own language.

"I hate to be insular," said Wyatt, "but would you

mind very much if we carried on our discussions in English?"

"Not at all," said Milanovitch with great restraint. "First of all, do you know this man, Inspector?"

"No. I think I know who he is, but we've never met."

"Then permit me to introduce you. Inspector Wyatt and Sergeant Tucker of the Metropolitan Police. Colonel Kosta, late of the Serbian War Ministry."

"Colonel," said Wyatt, bowing.

Kosta, who had regained his poise, returned Wyatt's bow. "It's a pleasure to meet you, Inspector. May I ask if this is an official visit?"

"It need not be. I'd like to talk to you for a few minutes, ask you a few questions. May we come in?"

Kosta looked at him sharply, and Wyatt was aware that a very keen mind was weighing a whole series of possibilities.

"Of course," he said, making a decision. "I'm not alone, but . . . Do come in."

He stepped aside politely, and when Wyatt, Tucker and the count had entered, he opened one of the large double doors that led to the front parlor. The entrance hall had been empty except for a console table and a single chair, and the parlor was sparsely furnished also. However the few pieces that were placed here and there about the large room were quite good. Sitting in a gilt chair near one of the windows that looked out onto the street was a woman in her late middle age, whose face was heavily powdered and who wore a rather ornate red wig.

"We have some unexpected guests," Kosta said to her. "Count Milanovitch of the Serbian Embassy just down the street, Inspector Wyatt and Sergeant Tucker of the Metropolitan Police. Mrs. Barnett."

"How do you do, Mrs. Barnett?" said Wyatt, bowing. "I've never had the pleasure of meeting either you or the late Mr. Barnett, but of course I've heard a good deal about you both."

"Only good, of course," she said, studying him with hard, dark eyes.

"Of course."

"I heard Colonel Kosta ask if you were here on official police business, and you said no."

"That's not quite accurate. He asked if this was an official visit, and I said that it need not be. That, if I might, I'd like to ask you a few questions."

"Me or the colonel?"

"Both of you."

"Well, seeing that the colonel is a foreigner and doesn't know as much about England and English law as me, why don't you start with me, and I'll decide if we'll answer your questions or not?"

"Fair enough. First of all, would you care to tell me what you're doing here?"

"You mean here in this house?"

"Yes."

"The colonel had business to take care of here in England. He got in touch with me and asked me to help him with it and to begin by finding him a house. I found this one for him."

"You know, of course, that the house is quite close to the Serbian embassy."

"Of course I know it. The colonel said he wanted to be near the embassy so that he could talk to the people there if he needed to."

"Then how is it that he never has?" asked the count. "I did not even know he was in England until a few minutes ago."

"I have only been here a short while, and I have not had a chance to pay my respects," said the colonel.

"You still haven't told us what this is all about, why you're asking us these questions," said Mrs. Barnett.

"Because I still have a few more questions to ask," said Wyatt. "Did you know that King Alexander was coming to England? That he was going to be staying at the embassy?"

"Of course we knew it," said Mrs. Barnett. "One of the reasons I came here today was because I hoped I might be able to see him."

"Well, you should be able to in just a minute. Because the carriage is waiting in front of the embassy now to take him to see the queen."

"No kid! Is that the truth?"

"It is."

"Hear that, Colonel?" Mrs. Barnett looked fixedly at him. "Sounds to me like this is a real occasion. Why don't you ring for Sam and have him bring up some bubbly?"

"Splendid idea." He went over to the bellpull that hung down the middle of the far wall. "You say he'll be along soon, Inspector?"

"He was getting ready to go when we left the embassy." Wyatt strolled over to the window and looked out. "Yes. He's coming out now, getting into the carriage."

"Let's see," said Mrs. Barnett. She got up, leaning on her silver-headed cane, and stumped over to stand next to Wyatt. " 'Strewth! There he is."

She watched the footman close the door of the brougham and climb up into the box, and Wyatt saw her lift a finger. As she did, out of the corner of his eye, he saw the colonel tug once on the bellpull.

With a clatter of hoofs, the brougham rolled by, and as they caught a fleeting glimpse of the young king, a little pale but very splendid in a full-dress uniform, she raised her finger again, and the colonel tugged on the bellpull for the second time.

Even Sargeant Tucker, standing in the doorway on the far side of the room, could feel the growing tension. Then, as the brougham went on up the street, as Mrs. Barnett lifted her finger again and the colonel tugged on the bellpull for the third time, both of them became rigid, crouching slightly as if waiting for something. Milanovitch, his lips a thin, tense line, stood in the middle of the room, frowning as if he did not understand what was going on.

They remained that way, all of them as rigid as wax figures at Madame Tussaud's for a long moment. Then Mrs. Barnett, her eyes wide and incredulous, turned and looked at the colonel, who was looking as astonished as she was.

"Is anything wrong?" asked Wyatt politely.

"Wrong?" said Mrs. Barnett, her voice hoarse and uncertain. "What could be wrong?"

"I think I can guess," said Wyatt. He nodded to Tucker, who went striding across the parlor to the dining room behind it. Zerko tried to stop him, but he shoved him aside, went around the screen at the end of the dining room, through the butler's pantry and pushed open the green baize door that closed off the back stairs. He paused there, looking down at the little man who crouched over a large storage battery, holding a wire to one of the terminals.

"Hello, Sam," he said. "Playing Hide and Seek?"

"What?" The small man looked up at him blankly, as uncomprehending as the colonel and Mrs. Barnett had been.

"Never mind. There's someone inside who wants to see you." And picking him up by the back of his jacket,

Tucker hustled him through the pantry and the dining room to the parlor.

"What was he doing?" asked Wyatt.

"Sitting on the back stairs, fiddling with the biggest blinking battery I've ever seen," said Tucker.

"Now will you tell us what this bobbery's all about?" said Mrs. Barnett.

"Why, yes," said Wyatt. "It's about an attempt to assassinate King Alexander by exploding a cache of dynamite in the sewer up the street."

"I knew it!" said the count. "At least, I began to suspect it after you came to see me this morning. Gradowsky is in it too, isn't he?"

"Yes."

"Was that what they were waiting for just now, when Kosta pulled the bellpull?"

"Yes. Three rings was evidently his signal to our friend here to set it off."

"But that's ridiculous!" said the colonel. "Why would we even try such a thing when you were here in the house?"

"An interesting question," said Wyatt. "And I wondered whether you *would* try. But of course you didn't know how much I knew and, being a pair of sporting types, decided to gamble on it. Your ace was probably the thought that when the dynamite went off, it would do so much damage, create so much confusion, that you could slip out the back way and scarper. But—" He broke off as Sam slid a hand inside his jacket and whipped out a long, slim knife. But, quick as he was, Tucker was just as quick.

"Now, now, none of that, Sammy," he said, clamping a hand on the small man's wrist. "You could hurt someone playing with that."

"We'll want that as evidence," said Wyatt as the knife fell to the floor. "It's undoubtedly the knife that killed Ernie the tosher and almost killed young Harry the bootblack."

"My daughter," said the count. "Do they have her?"

"Yes," said Wyatt.

"Where is she? Is she here in this house?"

"I'm not sure. She may be, but I doubt it."

Milanovitch walked over to the colonel. His face was expressionless, but his smoldering eyes were enough to make a very brave man draw back from him.

"Where is she, Kosta?" he said in a flat, uninflected voice. "Tell me, or I'll kill you."

The colonel was brave, there was little question about that, but there was uncertainty in his face as he looked at Addie Barnett, at Wyatt, and then at the count again.

"Don't look at them," said the count. "Look at me. You know I mean it. If you don't tell me where she is—or if she's been harmed in any way—I'll kill you as surely as I stand here. I may not be able to do it right away, but I'll do it—and you know I will."

Perspiration suddenly beaded the colonel's forehead,

and again he looked at Addie Barnett. She looked thoughtfully and speculatively at the count.

"She means a lot to you, eh?" The count did not even bother answering. "All right," she said, turning to Wyatt, "we'll do a deal with you. You can have Sam here. He did kill the tosher and the boy—at least he was supposed to —"

"What?" said Sam. "Why, you pongy, po-faced Judas!"

"Cut it. They got you, ain't they?" she said without emotion. "But, no matter what we tried, we didn't really do nothing. So, like I said, we'll do a deal with you, Inspector. Let us go, and we'll tell you where the girl is." Then, as Wyatt studied her, "Make your mind up fast, chum, because—this is gospel—if you don't get her right away, she's a goner!"

As Wyatt hesitated—and it was obvious that, much as he hated the idea, he was about to agree—the outside door burst open and Andrew came running into the room, followed by two panting policemen.

"Come on!" he said to Wyatt. "And hurry! I know where they are!"

"I'm sorry, sir," said one of the policemen to Wyatt. "You said no one was to come in, and I tried to stop him, but—"

"Stow it!" said Andrew, interrupting him. Then to Wyatt. "Didn't you hear me? I said I know where they are!"

"I heard you," said Wyatt. Then, to the two police-men, "Watch these four. They're under arrest. Come on," he said to Tucker and the count, and as Andrew went running out, they followed him. Tucker paused only long enough to wave to two additional police-men, who were waiting at the corner, indicating that they were to go into the house and help their colleagues. Then he went pounding up the street after Andrew, Wyatt and the count.

"Where are they?" asked Wyatt.

"There," said Andrew, pointing to a house several hundred yards farther up the street.

"How do you know?"

"Sara used a mirror to flash sun in my eyes."

It was typical of Andrew's feelings about Sara that he never doubted for a moment that it was she. And it was typical of Wyatt's attitude toward both of them, that he never asked Andrew how he knew it was Sara.

The house, more dilapidated and rundown than any near it, was on the other side of the street, next to an alley. They crossed the street, ran up the steps and tried the door. It was locked. As Andrew threw himself futilely against it, the count looked down into the area and went even whiter than he had been.

"Look!" he said, pointing down at the smoke that was beginning to puff out through the iron gate and from the cracks in the basement windows. "That woman! She said . . ."

Though he was unquestionably the strongest man there, Tucker did not even try the door. After one glance at it, he took out his whistle and blew three shrill blasts. The two men in the coal dealer's dray sat up, and when Tucker waved to them, the driver shook the reins and sent the dray rattling up the street toward them. Tucker went running down the steps to meet it.

"Give me a pinch bar quick!" he shouted.

Stopping in front of the house, one of the plain-clothesmen, dressed as a coal heaver, reached under the seat, brought out a short crowbar and threw it to Tucker. Then he took out an axe and a sledge hammer, and he and his mate started up the steps to join Tucker. But he needed no help. Driving the slightly bent chisel edge of the jemmy into the side of the door next to the knob, he surged against it. There was a splintering, snapping sound, and the door burst open. Smoke, curling up from below, was starting to fill the hallway, and not far off, they could hear the crackle of flames.

"Do you know where they are?" asked Wyatt.

"Yes. Attic. I'll show you," said Andrew, starting up the stairs.

The other house, number 169, seemed to have been sparsely furnished, but there was no sign of any furniture at all in this one. Racing up the stairs, Andrew went past room after empty room. Even where the doors were closed, he had a feeling that the rooms behind them were bare and unfurnished. By the time he reached the last, uncarpeted flight of stairs that led to the servant's quarters in the attic, his heart was pounding and he was panting. The stairs took him to a short, dusty corridor with one door opening off it. He turned the knob, threw himself against it, but the door did not open. He threw himself against it again, but it did not budge.

"It's locked!" he said to Wyatt, who had now joined him. "Did the sergeant bring up the pinch bar?"

"No," said Tucker, coming up the last flight of stairs with the count behind him. "But I don't need it. Stand back."

Bracing himself against the wall, he drove the heel of his heavy boot against the door with tremendous force. Again there was a splintering noise, and the door opened as the one below had done.

Andrew was the first one into the sparsely furnished attic room. A dark-haired girl whom he did not know was lying bound and gagged on one of the two cots. Sara, also bound and gagged, was lying in a heap on the floor. As he bent down, started to pick her up, she opened her eyes and looked at him.

"I'll take her," said Wyatt, pushing Andrew aside. "Tucker, get the other one."

"Got her," said the sergeant, picking up Maria. Then, as the count appeared in the doorway, "She's all right, sir. Now go on back down and out of here before we're all frizzled like kippers. Because this place is going up like a Guy Fawkes bonfire."

There was good reason for this exhortation, for the smoke was getting thicker and the crackling of flames louder. By the time they got downstairs they were all coughing, and Andrew's eyes were watering so that he could barely see. But one of the detectives dressed as a coal heaver stood in the hallway with a bandanna tied over his mouth and guided them out.

Tucker gave Maria to her father, who stood there hugging her, but Wyatt carried Sara across the street before he put her down. Andrew was trying to untie the cloth that was tied around her mouth when Tucker handed him his clasp knife. Andrew cut the cloth, cut the rope that tied her hands and feet and helped her sit up.

"Well," said Sara, spitting out her gag, "you sure took your blinking time finding me, didn't you?"

"I'm sorry," said Andrew.

"You should be! If you'd been copped and I'd been outside, I'll bet I'd have found you days ago!"

"I'm sure you would," said Andrew.

Then looking at his smoke-stained face, her eyes filled with tears, and as he put his arms around her, she buried her face against his chest.

16

The Two Recognitions

Young King Alexander's visit to Scotland Yard took place two days later, and it was, to begin with, fairly routine. He had asked if Sara and Maria, whom he had not yet met, could be there along with Andrew, and when they agreed, Count Milanovitch suggested that they all come to his house afterward to celebrate the king's escape from jeopardy and Maria's safe return. They all agreed to this too, though Wyatt was hesitant about it until the count assured him that though the king would be there also, it would all be very simple and informal.

They met at the Yard at three o'clock, and though Sara had not been drilled as intensively as Maria, when she was presented to the king, she gave him a splendid royal curtsey, one that Miss Fizdale would have been proud of. She and Maria were both understandably shy at first, but the young king was so warm and unaffected, so obviously interested in everything that Wyatt showed him, that by the time they left the Black Museum they were all chattering as if they had known one another for years.

Andrew's first suspicion that something out of the ordinary was about to happen came as they were preparing to leave. When they had first arrived at the Yard, the two constables who had been assigned to guard the king and went with him everywhere had remained at the entrance to the courtyard. Now there were a score or more policemen standing there as if they were waiting for something. At the same time, a small group of men had gathered near the building's main entrance. Andrew recognized at least two of them. One was Chadwick of the Foreign Office, and the other was someone he had not seen for some time.

"Isn't that Superintendent Wendell?" he asked Tucker, who was standing near him.

"Yes."

"Who's the grey-haired man with him?"

"The commissioner."

"What's he doing here?"

"I haven't a clue."

There was something so unconvincing about the way Tucker said this that Andrew turned to look at him and realized that Wyatt was staring at him too; but exhibiting a sudden absorption in a loose button on his coat sleeve, the sergeant avoided both their eyes. Looking again at the men who stood on the far side of the commissioner, the superintendent and Chadwick, Andrew saw that most of them had notebooks in their hands and realized that they must be reporters and that at least one of them was making a sketch of the Yard and all those in it.

It was at this moment, as Wyatt, looking stricken, tried to slip back into the building, that the king stepped forward and addressed him.

"Yes, Your Majesty?" said Wyatt.

"I have thanked you before, you and all those others gathered here who helped unravel and prevent the atrocious plot on my life. But words are not enough. And so, in the presence of representatives of your government and mine, of officials of your splendid police department and of your colleagues, I would like to present you with the highest honor my country can bestow, the Order of St. Simeon."

He turned to Count Milanovitch, who had produced a velvet-covered case and was holding it out to him. The king took out the decoration, an enameled and jewelled Maltese cross strung on a gold and purple ribbon. Wyatt, his face pale, bent his head, and as the king slipped the ribbon over it, all those in the courtyard, and particularly the constables, cheered.

"It is an honor I will always treasure, Your Majesty," said Wyatt. "Thank you." Then, in a lower voice, "I don't have to wear it now, do I?"

"No," said the king, smiling. "Give him the box, Michael. But I shall expect you to wear it when you come to dinner at the embassy and when you come to visit me in Serbia."

Then, as Chadwick, the commissioner and the superintendent came over to congratulate Wyatt and to talk to the king, Andrew said to Tucker, "You knew about it, didn't you?"

"Yes. They twigged he wouldn't like it, so they told me not to say anything about it. But they said it was very important, not just for the inspector and the Yard, but for relations between us and the king's country."

"It sounds like a Foreign Office do. And of course that's why the press is here."

Tucker nodded. And it was then, as the journalists came forward to talk to Wyatt and the king, that Andrew and the sergeant saw someone else who had been standing behind them, General Wyatt.

"Good afternoon, sir," said Andrew. "I'm sorry, but I didn't see you before. Have you been here long?"

"About ten minutes."

"More of your work, Sergeant?" asked Andrew.

"You mean, did he suggest that I come here?" said the general. "No. I came entirely by accident. It's been several days since I was here last, and—"

He broke off as Wyatt, hearing his voice, turned and saw him.

"Father!"

"Good afternoon, Peter."

Again Wyatt looked sharply at Tucker, glanced once more at his father, then made up his mind.

"Your Majesty," he said, "may I present my father, General Wyatt?"

"Your father?" said the young king, turning to the erect, white-haired man. "I'm delighted to meet you, General." Then, with great warmth, "You must be very proud of your son."

"I am," said the general simply.

"Of course, you know Commissioner Clyde of the Metropolitan Police."

"I'm afraid I don't."

"Allow me the pleasure of presenting you," said the king, and taking the general by the arm, he began introducing him to the commissioner, the superintendent and all the others who surrounded them.

A third time Wyatt looked at Tucker, a dour, dire look.

"He didn't do it," said Sara. "Tell your father about all this, I mean."

"Is that what he told you?"

"Yes. And he wouldn't lie about it."

"Not even if he knew I was considering having him transferred to foot patrol on the Isle of Dogs?"

"I might," said Tucker. "But as it happens, I didn't tell him about it. If you don't believe me, you can ask the old gentleman himself."

Wyatt grunted, and as he glanced at the general, standing there next to the king, Count Milanovitch, who had been with them, approached them.

"As you've no doubt noticed," he said, "His Majesty is greatly taken with your father and has invited him to join us at my place. I'm sure you have no objection to that."

"No," said Wyatt. "I've no objection."

The general's hearing must have been very good or very discriminating, for in spite of the talk that was going on around him, he glanced at Wyatt.

"Are you sure, Peter?" he asked.

"Yes, father."

"Then . . . I don't know how much longer you plan to stay here, but my carriage is waiting on the Embankment, and I'll be glad to take you to the count's house—you, your two young friends and Sergeant Tucker."

"I could do without Sergeant Tucker very nicely, but . . . Very well. I've had enough of the hooraw here. I'm ready to go now."

"Splendid." And with military skill and diplomatic finesse, the general effected a disengagement and led his party out through the gate to the Embankment.

"There's just one thing," said Wyatt as the coachman opened the carriage door and stood there at attention. "I'd like to stop for a moment on Dover Street."

"Just give Perkins the address," said the general. "In

you go, miss," he said, helping Sara in.

They were all silent for a few moments after the carriage started. Then, somewhat tentatively, the general said, "I hope you'll forgive me, but I'm afraid I don't know the details of the exploit that lies behind that ceremony at the Yard. I gather you did something quite remarkable, Peter."

"It wasn't remarkable at all," said Wyatt.

"Of course not," said Sara scornfully. "He does that sort of thing every day and twice on Sunday."

"What sort of thing?"

"Rescuing the count's daughter and me from kidnappers and saving the king from being blown to kingdom come."

"That's enough, Sara," said Wyatt.

"Not half, it's not! After all, a lot of it happened to me, and I got a right to talk about it if I want to." Then, as Wyatt half-rose, fumbling with the door handle, "Sergeant, you're bigger than he is. Can't you keep him quiet while I tell the general about it?"

"I'll try. After all, it is all going to be in the newspapers, sir."

"But I won't have to listen to what they say," said Wyatt.

"Then don't listen," said Sara and launched into a graphic, but on the whole accurate, account of what had happened.

"There's just one thing I don't understand," said Andrew. "Why did they need two houses, one on Claverton Street and one just off it?"

"Think!" said Wyatt. "I can tell you that Colonel Kosta leased the one off Claverton Street about a month ago, shortly after he came to London, and Addie took the other one just a few days ago."

"Of course," said Andrew. "Kosta needed a place immediately in which to keep Maria and, as it happened, Sara. But it was only after they had gotten the count out of the way and learned what route the king was going to take to Buckingham Palace that they knew where to place the dynamite and therefore where the second house had to be."

"Exactly. Apparently Kosta had worked out the broad outline of the plot before he came here. But he needed someone with a specialized knowledge of London criminals and, as it happened, of sewer workers to establish the details. That's why he got in touch with Addie Barnett."

"Well, I must say I think that what you did was remarkable. And when I say you, I mean all of you," said the general, looking around the carriage. "And of course now I understand why you haven't had a chance to do anything about the problem I presented you with, Peter."

"You mean finding Harriet."

"Yes. Why are we stopping?" he asked as the carriage

drew up in front of a sober brownstone townhouse. "Oh. Is this the address you wanted?"

Wyatt glanced at the bronze plaque next to the door, which identified the building as the Twelfth Night Club, and nodded.

"I shouldn't be more than a few minutes," he said, opening the carriage door. "Would you like to come in with me, sir?"

"Me? Why should I?"

"You might find it interesting."

"If you say so," said the general stepping out of the carriage after him. "What sort of club is it?"

"I'm not sure," said Wyatt. "I'll enquire."

They entered the club, which seemed particularly quiet and sedate. Wyatt approached the uniformed porter at the desk and talked to him for a moment. The porter nodded and went off along the corridor that led to the club's public rooms, and Wyatt returned to the general.

"It's a woman's club," he said.

"I gather you didn't know that."

"No. I suspected it, but didn't know for sure."

"I wouldn't dream of criticizing your methods if this is a police matter, Peter—not after the success you've just had—nor your manners, if it's social, but may I say that I find this rather odd? You come here, to a place you apparently don't know, I assume to meet someone—"

"Let's say, rather, that I came here hoping to find someone."

"But who? And why did you think I might be interested? After all—"

He broke off, staring, as the porter came back down the corridor, followed by a slim and attractive young woman.

"Harriet!"

"Hello, Father. Hello, Peter," she said. "I must say it took you longer to find me than I thought it would."

"As it happens, I could have done so almost immediately," said Wyatt, "but I've been rather busy. And besides, I saw no particular need to hurry."

She stared at him, startled and a little disconcerted.

"No need?"

"Just a second," said the general. "Are you saying you knew where she was all along?"

"It depends on what you mean by all along. Her letter told me a good deal, and the visit to her room told me everything else I needed to know."

"What? But you only saw the letter once. I've had it all along and read it many times, and I didn't find anything in it . . ."

"We don't read things in quite the same way. Was there any mention of me in the letter?"

"No."

"Then why did you come to me?"

"Well, we may not have been on good terms, but I

knew you liked Harriet and finding people is part of your job."

"Which the letter went out of its way to remind you of when it spoke of Scotland Yard. It was fairly clear to me that what Harriet was saying was, 'All of Scotland Yard might not be able to find me, but one person there might.' "

"Bravo," said Harriet. "That's just what I meant."

"Once I decided that she wanted me involved, the rest was easy. Did you recognize the final quotation in which she talked of sitting like Patience on a monument, smiling at grief?"

"I'm not sure. Shakespeare, isn't it?"

"Yes. From *Twelfth Night*. I seemed to recall that she had stayed at a club here before she and Francis were married, and I also had a feeling that I'd heard of a club by that name."

"I see. But why did she do it?"

Wyatt glanced at Harriet, but she shook her head.

"You're doing very well. You might as well finish."

"There was a book of poems on her desk. Do you remember whose they were?"

"William Blake's."

"Yes. Did you, by any chance, read the poem she had marked with a bookmark?"

"No."

"You might have found it significant. It was from his *Songs of Innocence*, and it went:

'*Can I see another's woe*
And not be in sorrow too?
Can I see another's grief
And not seek for kind relief?' "

"I see," said the general. "At least . . ."

"You know how I feel about the way you've been be-having, Father," said Harriet. "I think you've been very unfair to Peter, and I just couldn't go off to India and leave things the way they were. So I thought if I disap-peared and you were concerned enough to go to Peter and ask him to help you find me . . ."

"Yes," said the general. "I understand."

"I'll accept the fact that you've been busy," she said to Peter, "but why did you also say that you saw no particular need to hurry?"

"Well, first of all, I knew that you had at least three more days before you had to leave for India. And second, while I knew what you were doing and why, I wasn't sure I approved of your interfering."

"Oh," said Harriet. "I'm sorry."

"No," said the general. "I'm the one who's sorry. I have been for some time, since almost immediately after I got so furious at you for joining the police. I knew I was being narrow-minded, bigoted and snobbish, but along with all my other bad qualities, I also happen to be very stubborn—"

"Please, Father—"

"Will you be quiet?" said the general forcefully. "If I want to apologize to you, I'm going to!"

"No, you're not," said Wyatt just as firmly. "I don't want to hear your apology!"

They scowled at one another, and it was the general who gave way.

"Very well, Peter," he said. He held out his hand, and Wyatt took it.

"Am I forgiven?" asked Harriet in a small voice.

"Oh, my dear," said the general, putting an arm around her. "It's not a matter of forgiving, but of thanking, commending and even acclaiming. Do you agree, Peter?"

"Why, yes. I might even agree to let her come with us when we leave here. Would you like to meet a very charming sixteen-year-old king, Harriet?"

"Is that one of your police jokes?" she asked.

"No, my dear," said the general. "It's one of the results of Peter's latest exploit, which you'll read about in tomorrow's newspapers. And I think you should come with us. We'll be a little crowded in the carriage . . ."

"No, we won't," said a voice behind them. "Not if Andrew sits up in the box with Perkins."

They turned to see Sara and Andrew standing just inside the club entrance.

"Is that what you came in to tell us?" asked Wyatt.

"Yes," said Sara.

"Just a second," said the general. "Are you going to tell me that you knew that Harriet was here, too?"

"Of course," said Sara.

"How?"

"Well, we knew you had asked the inspector to find her," said Andrew. "And we also knew that he'd been too busy to do anything about it up to now. But when he said he wanted to stop here, we were sure it was because she was here."

"I see," said the general. "It seems that your powers of deduction have been passed on to another generation, Peter. And it also seems as if only I, of all those who know you, had any doubts about your infallibility. From now on I shall, of course, be numbered among your unquestioning supporters. As for you, Andrew, by all means sit in the box. And tell Perkins I said that, if you wish, you may even handle the ribbons."